Bare Feet and Creek Rocks

Based on a True Story

Joann Browning

ISBN: 979-8-89212-606-9

Dedication

Dear Mom,

I dedicate this story to you, Linda, and to your empire.

I want to thank you and Dad for allowing us to grow, seek, explore, and learn through adventure rather than a long list of rules. Through that, I believe we were able to find our own path, confront our own fears, and realize just how strong we are.

With all the love,

Sincerely,

Your daughter,

Joann

Acknowledgment

Special thanks to:

Billy Joe Browning for providing the title to this story.

Darrell Wyatt for listening and patience of the many hours I needed for completion.

Len Tully for inspiration on this project to pursue to the end.

Donna Browning for the support.

Taylor Stewart for all the help when all my writing was lost.

About the Author

My name is Joann Browning, and my 61 years of life have consisted of great times, hard times, and idle times like many in my world. Out of high school, I focused on a career path where I spent 21 years in corporate production management. Then my father fell ill and needed me. I found myself needing him more at the time due to my own trials. After his passing, I focused on a less stressful and demanding career path to find balance in my life. I currently reside just south of my infamous creek in an adjoining waterway where my heart and soul were raised.

I am a daughter, a sister, a mother, a grandmother, a companion, and friends with many. I divide my time between my hometown of Hamilton, Ohio, where I currently work for a cleaning company, and the Lake Cumberland, Ky. Burnside area, where I focused on writing this story.

Preface

A little over nine years ago, I was staring at yet another life-changing event. Per my mother's request, I tasked myself to write this story.

I tried to capture innocence, simplicity, and challenge during a time not complicated with modern technology and society's fast and ever-changing world. Our evolving world has moved at a pace where many old standards of humanity are being cast away for just mere compliance.

I tried to write some in between the lines of this story and capture a truly enjoyable journey along the way.

Contents

Introduction

As years pass, people can find themselves caught up in the same routine of life until it is all turned upside down. It cannot be fixed, and it will never be the same now. We just adjust, adapt, and move on from there.

The pain of losing someone close to you does not get easier as we age, but we somehow learn to deal with it. Why? Is it because we know our time left on Earth gets shorter each day? Does time and faith give us comfort knowing that we will meet again?

Due to the eighteen-year age difference between my parents, I was too young to realize the pain my father felt as he lost his parents, brothers, sisters, and friends throughout his life. Even when he lost two of his eleven children in a car accident, I was just saddened while he was tormented. However, when his time came, he was at peace.

I am seeing the same in my mother. She has now lost her parents, siblings, a husband, two of her children, and soon a third. She is dealing with it, and with time and a belief in a heavenly reunion, the pain will ease.

They all leave us with memories—good, bad, happy, or sad. We struggle with our families, jobs, and relationships, yet we find the power to go on because they visit our memories from time to time. Even in our darkest moments, they help us to smile from within.

Present Day

I held my sister Linda's hand, refusing to let go, as I scanned the small room, wishing for another chance to go fishing. Her daughters were complete opposites of one another, yet both were broken. One was saddened and searching for calm, while the other was on a mission to fix the system their mother was in. Together, though, they were one. Her four grandchildren, protected from the pain by their young ages and innocence, added some energy to the room. Her devoted and loving husband, Gary, has since turned his anger at providence to submission, then acceptance, and now his face shows it, sad yet graceful.

Mom kisses her daughter's cheek and says, "You are my best friend," as tears stream down her face. Her voice was strong and steady, refusing to show weakness.

"I love you, Mom," comes the weak reply. "I'm okay."

I hold my sister's hand into the wee hours that night, talking and laughing with her. Our exhausted mother gets up from her chair, raises her hand, and waves as if to brush us off.

"Those two are still up to no good," she says to everyone in the room. "I'm going to go lay down."

A few hours later, my sister fell asleep, and with hesitation, I released her hand. It would be the last I would feel life as I knew it. Her life. Forever. It was dreary that early morning when I drove home, realizing that life, as it is, is broken and cannot ever be fixed. I will have to face my big sister's passing within the hours. During that drive, however, I remember...

Chapter 1

Flashback to June 1971

Millville, Ohio

The yellow school bus's brakes screeched as it came to a stop. The doors opened, and we jumped off. With a short wave to Mr. Kunkle and those left on the bus, Danny, Linda, Vickie, and I took off down the seemingly mile-long gravel lane that sat between two cornfields. It rained earlier, so we had to dodge the mud holes as we ran home. My feet thumping from a whole day at school in my hard shoes, I ran down the lane. The corn was already as high as our heads but would soon grow to become a wall for the summer. Passing the small wood of trees, we rounded the curve in the lane where we could see our house.

A small, light gray, four-bedroom block house sat tucked in behind a grove of blackberry and raspberry vines just past a big sycamore we called the "three trees." Floor rugs were draped over a wire fence with a single strand of barbwire that stretched along the whole length of the yard where another field of corn was growing. On the other side of the lane, next to the depleted stack of coal, was Dad's work stuff. A collection of cars and lawnmowers he worked on for side money.

A two-story house had stood there once. From what I remember, Dad had rented the house to a lady with two teenage boys. We had gotten a new cow, and Danny, Linda, and I were atop the outbuilding, looking down at it through the top of the door. One of the boys purposely slammed the door shut and smashed our fingers. This angered Dad, and he later evicted them from the home. Dad could not handle a kid being hurt, especially by the hand of another. After they moved out, Dad stepped onto the wooden porch to see what condition the house was left in, and a nail went through his work boot and into his foot. Angry, he burnt it down, and the outside grill made of creek rock was all that remained.

A big steelwork table and chain hoist hung from a locust tree where he could work in the shade. Many different building materials lay strewn about and stacked up that he earned from trading out car work. He planned on using them to build an addition to the house or to sell and trade.

The dollar wasn't as important to Dad as a man's honesty and a fair deal. Knowing he helped someone in need was usually payment enough, and he believed it would pay off in the end, yet any man should not wear out his welcome.

Planter boxes lay empty, and the hinged glass panels rested against the hunter-green chicken coop to keep them from getting broken. All the plants had already been transplanted in the garden. A high, white, slatted fence pen surrounded the coop, which was full of chickens and a mean rooster. Beyond the fenced pen, a weathered outhouse stood. A large stack of cement blocks rested in the weeds for an addition to the house. Grandma and Grandpa would be coming in soon from Hazard, Kentucky, to start the foundation for it.

A U-shaped stack of blocks for a fire sat near a short crabapple tree. It was used to heat water in a washtub for canning and processing chickens. The tree provided a nice shade spot for working, and the kids enjoyed climbing into it. A potato patch was already taking shape behind the coop and beyond the tall weeds, and a line of trees was a small creek. A small road led down to the creek at the curve in the lane, but we would just follow a footpath through the weeds and trees to get to it.

The backyard was filled with clotheslines, and a ringer washer sat by the backdoor. Past the walnut and peach trees were two fenced-in pens and two outbuildings, where we had pigs and cows that we raised for food. Along the tree row, next to the creek, the garden had already been tilled and planted with sweet corn, beans, cabbage, tomatoes, peppers, and cucumbers, which we would pick when ready for canning.

Our house was small for eleven children. A coal stove sat in the light pink, almost white, rippled paneled walls of the living room and displayed soiled hand marks from the children at every door edge. A large console TV sat at an angle in the corner for easy viewing. The couch and chair had recently been replaced after Linda sliced her knee open from a wire sticking out from one of the arms of the old couch. The material had worn thin due to all the children learning to walk, and for that reason, the coffee table was history years ago. Two end tables with lamps were tucked in close to the couch and chair so the smaller children didn't fall and get hurt.

The kitchen was small because of the huge freezer chest for food that doubled as counter space. Next to it, a few cartons of empty pop bottles rested for return, along with a large collection of folded brown grocery bags. The stove, a deep double sink in a white metal cabinet, and the loud well pump finished the wall. Three bookcase-style shelves were inset, high in the wall, and filled with canned goods so the jars would not get broken with us playing hopscotch on the black and white tiled floor. The chimney to the coal stove was encased in blocks here and created a catchall for the large bags of potatoes and onions.

A metal frame table with six chairs sat in the center of the room. White metal cabinets hung high on the walls next to the block chimney, and an additional set above the freezer and stove. Dishes, cereal, and canned goods were difficult for us to reach, and dragging a metal chair to stand on throughout the kitchen and/or lifting a smaller child up to get what we needed was commonplace. The refrigerator had a hasp on the door; my guess was so the smaller children didn't crawl inside or maybe to keep us from getting in it all the time, or we simply wore the latch out. It sat next to the side door that usually had a baby bed blocking it during the day. Mom could tend to the baby more easily while working in the kitchen.

In the bathroom, a white wicker clothes hamper stayed full of dirty clothes to be washed daily. The lower slats of its white louvered door were bowed out from the smaller children asking us older ones for things through the door.

The back bedroom had a set of wooden bunk beds without a ladder because it was not needed. The children, once old enough, would climb the end of the bed like a tree to get to the top to sleep. A treadle sewing machine sat next to a back door. Mom would use it for making and mending our clothes or sewing scraps together for quilts. Laundry baskets filled with play clothes, underwear, and towels sat next to the bathroom door. An ironing board and a clothes rack for school clothes sat next to the hot water heater, which was too small for all of us at bath time.

Mom and Dad's bedroom had a large bed, a small closet, a baby bed, and a chest of drawers for the baby's clothes. A rollaway bed sat folded up against the wall and, at night, was moved into the living room for sleeping. For years, there was always a baby sleeping in there, so we never cut through the room.

There were no doors, except for the bathroom and their closet, which worked well for heating the house in the winter. At night, after watching some black and white TV or listening to Dad play the guitar, we all found a place to sleep, doubling up in the beds until we grew older. I think we were always too tired to care.

As we approached the house, the front door stood open, as always, and the gold-colored curtains were pulled back in the large crank-out front window. Mom was inside, probably tending to one of our baby brothers, David, who turned one in March, or Billy Joe, being just a month old. The rest of our sisters, Roberta "Gertie" (we would eventually call her "Berta" for short), Reva "Zam Zam," Pamela (Dad never cared for the name, so we always called her "Bam"), Kay "Spunky," and Donna were playing in the front yard where Mom would keep an eye on all of them.

Wearing only underwear and their faces dusty from dirt, Kay and Donna sat playing with old pots, pans, and spoons while the others ran up to greet us. The front yard, close to the house, never really grew grass and was always littered with bits of paper and cups. We played there so much it would not grow and was as hard as concrete.

The yard along the fence line displayed a small permanent baseball diamond layout, and a steel-frame picnic table Dad had made from metal pipes sat under a shady spot of locust trees. Many pink and white peony flowers lined the fence row up to the “three trees.” Nonetheless, it was home, tucked back away from everyone, and everything we needed was there.

The older kids, Danny and Linda, took care of us, and Mom managed the others. Danny was eleven and a half, while Linda had turned ten in February. I was eight, and Vickie was seven and a half years old.

After a quick hello to our sisters, we ran inside and slid our old school workbooks and supplies under the bunk bed. We would drag them out on rainy days and play school with the others. We changed out of our school clothes, picking through the laundry baskets and grabbing whatever fit. We took off our shoes and threw them under the couch. We wouldn’t be wearing them much at all over the summer, and one of the other kids would more than likely grow into them. All of us girls were about a year apart in age, so we got plenty of use out of our things.

We made our own peanut butter and jelly sandwiches to hold us over since Mom had her hands full with all the other kids all day. She had just started preparing dinner for Dad, who would be coming home from work soon.

The year was 1971, the school was finally out, and our full-day summer adventures were soon to begin.

Chapter 2

Linda and I spent hours convincing Mom to let us go upstream the night before. With school finally being out, we would have all day. We had spent most of our evenings and weekends planting in the garden and doing the extra laundry for school, among many other household chores. Now that Billy Joe was on somewhat of a schedule, she agreed to let us stay gone all day, well up to dinnertime. Danny said he would stay back to tinker with something like he usually did every day, and Mom said Vickie and Roberta could help with the other children and laundry.

We woke up early since we were still used to getting up for school and hurried to do our chores as fast as we could. Still foggy outside, Danny and Linda headed to the barns to feed the pigs and cows while I fed the chickens and collected the eggs. I checked the big red setting hen and her eggs since they would be hatching soon.

Wiping our feet off in the wet, dewy grass before going in the side door, we quietly grabbed a quick bowl of cereal, emptying the box; I pulled the box top off to save for a mail-order "Finger Ding" doll. We made our peanut butter sandwiches for the day and stuffed them into an empty bread bag to keep them dry. We grabbed an old coffee cup with a chip in the rim for our drinking water later in the spring while the others still slept.

Linda and I took off down the footpath with our cane poles in hand and bare feet. Linda batted at the spider webs with her pole that laced across our path as we made our way to the creek. We walked toward the water's edge and ran down the small hill over a small sandbar to the rocky creek bank.

The creek cut along a line of farm fields with high banks on the far side. Rough-winged swallows would bore holes in these soft dirt banks to lay their eggs in the early spring, and from the chirping sounds, their babies were just learning to fly. Every spring, the creek would flood due to heavy rains and wash gravel and rocks in, changing our swimming spots. Sometimes, trees washed in or fell. We wanted to explore further, and the water was finally getting warm enough to wade or swim in all day.

I noticed the water lay still as the fog rose from it, and the water spiders danced across the top. I had gotten eyeglasses a few months earlier and was amazed at how clear things finally were.

We took a short glance at the big hole of water and figured we could check it later as we walked along the edge; we were heading upstream. We crossed the rapids, which were just ankle-deep, and the gravel riddled in between the rocks made it easy to cross. We were glad to see our crossing spot had not changed after the spring floods.

We checked our spring water pipe, which was still shoved into the gray clay bank and had a good, steady stream of water pouring out and trickling through the rocks into the creek. We hung our cup on the pipe and left our sandwiches there, twisting the bread bag around a small sapling nearby. There was no reason to carry them around all day, and we would head back when we started getting hungry anyway.

A couple of large trees lay along the rocky bank left from the floods; we would check the large branches another time to see if they had any spring to them. If they did, we could bring some of the smaller children up to ride them. They tired easily and would be close to home.

We noticed the many rock bass running the waist-high water up to the next crossing point as we walked the water's edge, catching crawdads for bait, flipping over rocks, and with a swift hand, grabbing them before they could swim into the deeper water. We ran across batches and batches of tadpoles as we threw our lines in here and there, trying to catch bass as we made our way up the stream. We came up to the next set of rapids; these were getting a little bit harder to cross. The water was deeper, almost to our knees, and the rocks were larger and slick.

Stepping onto slick rocks, Linda and I both fell in, the water pushing us a little downstream before we could collect ourselves and get to the other side. The water seemed warm compared to the morning air as we stood wringing the excess water from our clothes. It was going to be a hot day, and I figured they would dry rather quickly.

On the way back, however, we could try to cross just in front of the slick rocks, but the water was waist-deep and had more force as the channel narrowed. Or we could try stepping on the rocks with the grassy moss. We did determine this spot would be a challenge for the smaller children to cross. But as the creek level lowered during the summer from lack of rain, we could pair up and get them to the other side without a problem.

We walked the bank edge for a while through a patch of what we called "saw grass" since it would cut your legs like a razor if you didn't step on it at the base and lay it down.

It stretched a good length along the spot and was soft on our feet after walking so long on the creek rocks. The bank dropped off where the creek had cut, and the water was about chest deep and calm, and the bottom was sandy.

On the other side, a large honey suckle tree lay in the water, having been washed from the bank, and a row of trees provided shade over the water. This looked like a nice place to fish in the late summer. The water would be lower by then, and we could wade in to fish.

The string on our poles was just too short to get close enough, and we would have to carry our bait. Linda and I talked about how only the big kids would be able to swim here until then due to the drop-off.

The creek forked at this point, and looking up the channel, you could see white caps of water rolling over the large rocks that had washed in. We never went up that channel. It was too dangerous, but if we had a cashing reel, we knew we could catch bass there. We always walked the dried rock bed on the other side, which water only ran through shortly after a flood and had since dried up.

The small saplings lay over from the force of the past flood waters, and the big balls of leaves, sticks, and mud caught in their branches weighed them down. We crossed over a small sandbar to a place we called "the turtle pond."

We knew it was too dangerous to swim here. An old farmer's junkyard of machinery lined the bank, and the flood water would eddy here, creating two muddy water holes. Only turtles and frogs lived in here, but occasionally, fish would get trapped after a flood, so it was worth checking. We decided to venture on after throwing our lines in a few times. We had not walked any farther than the turtle pond in the past, and this being the start of the summer, we craved more things and places to entertain all of us. Besides, we were older.

Chapter 3

We walked on up and found a farmer's tractor road that crossed over to the other side of the creek just ahead of the rough rapids. Linda decided she wanted to explore that side of the road. As long as the water wasn't too rough or high, we could probably cross here. We laid our poles off the side of the road and hid them behind a clump of sawgrass in case a farmer actually used this road. We had not been over to that side, and we needed to see. Besides, it was still early morning, and we knew our way.

We crossed the creek easily and followed the road just up the slight hill.

Linda said in a whisper, "Lay down, in case someone lives up here." So, we lay down in the tall field grass along the side of the road to ensure no one would see us.

Peeking above the grass into the distance, I saw grassy fields that seemed to go on forever with fences and buildings just like what we had at home. I saw a large cluster of cows grazing atop a hill in the distance, and the best thing ever was that I didn't see a farmer or a house. We were told not to mess with people's things, especially their gardens.

Linda said, "Come on," as she stood up.

I argued with her about going farther up, but I admit I was curious, too. This was not a garden or a planted crop field, and we know how to climb fences without breaking them down. We wouldn't undo the gates, and if we saw the farmer, we would just take off running back to the creek. Besides, he would never catch us, and he didn't know who we belonged to. We had a plan.

We walked the tractor road and saw two piles of old farm stuff pitched off to the side. We decided we could look at it later. Along the creek bed, a grove of trees stood with large jungle vines dressed throughout; we could swing on them another time. It was very shady here and would provide comfort from the sun on the upcoming summer days. We came up to a large metal farm gate and crawled under it. We looked through an old outbuilding just past the gate, and from the manure piles and the hair caught on the nails, we knew it was for cows. We had two cows at home, but there were a lot of them here, and they were much larger than ours.

We walked up a way, following a cow path leading atop a hill, and found a large farm pond. You could see where the cow's feet pierced the mud along the edges while drinking from it. Large bullfrogs jumped in as we circled the pond, only wondering if there were any fish in it since we had left our poles behind.

The cows had since moved closer to the outbuilding and stopped next to a hayrack and salt block. As we sat atop the hill resting and watching them, Linda noticed one with the longest set of horns we had ever seen. They stuck out about two feet on each side of his head and curled forward.

Linda said, "I watched on TV that if you waved your shirt like a rug at that kind of cow and yelled, 'Andale, Andale!' it would be kind of like dancing with you. You could keep on doing it back and forth till the cow got tired, and then, you would be able to pet it."

Her determination to make any animal a pet was astounding. She was thinking of a matador at the time, yet I imagined a coyote being smashed by an “Acme” brand rock, as I had seen on the Looney Tunes cartoons.

I said, “You are crazy. I don’t want to pet it. If you're going to try it, I'm getting on the other side of the fence.” I couldn’t run as fast as her due to some knee surgery I had a few years earlier; besides, her idea was just plain ridiculous.

We walked off the grassy hill to the fence, where I crossed back over as she walked toward that huge cow.

Taking her shirt off and shaking it, she yelled, “Andale! Andale!”

That cow turned his head and looked at her, waving her shirt, and with a big snort, he pawed the ground. As he took off, clumps of grass went flying, and he came charging at her. She spun around, her eyes as big as saucers, and she took off running to the fence, throwing her shirt atop the barbwire, and with one leap, she was over it! I reached up to help her, but as her body hit mine, we both rolled to the ground.

Luckily, the cow had just stopped short of the fence. He was breathing so hard you could feel the heat coming from his nose as we looked up at him. We both jumped up, screaming. With our hearts pumping so hard we could feel it in our throats, we ran as fast as we could down that road to the creek’s edge before we stopped.

After catching our breath and putting her shirt back on, Linda said, “I guess that one’s not tired,” then cupped her hands and scooped up a handful of water from the creek to drink.

We laughed and laughed at each other. I laughed at how scared she looked and how that cow nearly horned her in the behind. She laughed at me for trying to catch her in midair. We crossed the creek, picked up our poles, and made our way toward home, reminding each other not to tell Mom. Mom didn't need to know all the stupid things we did together.

We stopped at the spring and ate our sandwiches, still laughing and planning our next trip up to the pond with the other kids. It was very pretty up there, and there was a lot more to explore. We still wanted to play on the large vines hanging from the trees and look through those piles of junk. But the next time, we would definitely be leaving the cows alone.

We did some more fishing and checked the washed-up trees that lay on the bank. The branches were nice and strong but too long; they had too much spring. You couldn't ride them very long without falling off and hitting the rock bed underneath. Once was enough for me; it definitely hurt. After catching my wind back and realizing I didn't want to break my glasses, we couldn't bring a kid home to Mom with their head split open or a broken arm, so we canceled the idea of playing on that tree.

We crossed back over at our shallow crossing and checked the waterhole by our footpath before heading up to the house. The spring floods had washed a large boulder into our swimming hole and messed up our jumping spot. We could still swim and jump from the bank if someone sat on the rock to ensure no one hit it. Hopefully, the next flood would wash the rock downstream.

When we made it back to the house, Dad was home from work, and it was dinnertime. After dinner, we cleaned up the dishes and went outside to pull weeds in the garden. A big farm tractor came around the curve in the lane. It drove to where Dad was working and stopped; an old man wearing bib overalls and a straw hat looked small on that large Farmall M tractor as he sat there talking to Dad for a while.

Then Dad yelled, "Linda 'Sissy' and Joann 'Pebs,' get over here and meet this man."

Looking at each other, we brushed the dirt from our hands and walked over to them.

He said, "This man's name is Stanley Walter. He lives at the big farmhouse across the road, and he owns that big cow Sissy outran today," as he pointed in the direction of the cornfield next to the yard.

With a chuckle, the farmer said, "I have never seen anyone run so fast and scale a fence in one leap in my life. You ran as fast as a deer and jumped as high as one, too!" as he pointed to Linda.

We had forgotten all about looking for the farmer. He was up there somewhere and somehow saw us. We knew for sure we were in big trouble, but they both just laughed. We already knew not to do that again. That big cow nearly killed us.

Since then, we called the pond on the hill "Walter's Pond." We would see him riding his tractor from time to time, and he would always give us a nice wave. We never bothered him, knowing he was busy, but I know he would laugh remembering Linda trying to pet that big old cow.

Chapter 4

After spending the latter half of the morning swimming and playing at the creek with all the kids, except the baby, Billy Joe, we went on up to the house for lunch. Mom would make us all stay outside while she mopped the floors and made the beds; besides, it was a beautiful day. Sitting under the shade trees at the picnic table, eating bologna sandwiches, the old neighbor man named Dave Hall drove down in an old dark blue GMC truck, late 50s model, and stopped close to where Danny was working on a car for Dad.

He was a slim, frail-looking, elderly man and would occasionally dump his burnt trash, mostly broken glass and metal cans, into a hole Dad had dug, which would be covered later, in the wooded patch just beyond the curve. Danny had helped him repair his tiller a few months back so he could get his garden in on time.

He said he was having trouble with his lawnmower and asked Danny if he could come on up to look at it. Danny was good at fixing mowers and tillers and was getting even better at fixing cars. Grabbing a few tools, Danny headed up the lane, and Linda and I walked with him. We crossed the street at the top of the hill by the mailbox, and I mailed the order for my doll.

While Danny worked on the mower, Linda and I met the two girls who lived in the above apartment of the big white house. One of the girls was my age, eight and a half, and the other girl was close to Reva's age, five and a half. The older girl went to a different school than us, and we saw her waiting for her school bus in the morning from time to time.

We followed the girls down a sidewalk that led to the back side of the house and up to their front door. The door allowed access to a large, dark wooden staircase that led to the living area of the apartment. We went upstairs, and the girls showed us to their bedroom and their many Barbies. I sat down on the dark hardwood floor between two twin beds made up of frilly bedspreads to play with dolls and their many clothes with the younger girl.

Linda glanced at their toys and things and walked over to the bedroom window to look out.

She said to the older girl, "Look how high up we are. Everything is so small. Show me around."

After a short time, the girls seemed to be a bit nervous and asked us politely to leave before their mother got home. I got the impression that she was a very religious lady from the pictures on the walls. They were not allowed to have guests while their parents weren't home, or they would be grounded, whatever that meant. The girls invited us back to play as long as their parents were home. We were confused as to why their mother worked and drove a car, but we never asked.

We got up to leave, and as we exited, we heard arguing coming from the front side of the house. Danny had fixed the old man, Dave's mower, by then, and they were arguing about payment. Apparently, after Danny got done fixing the mower, he wanted Danny to go back to our house to bring back a quart of oil for the mower for a dime. Yes, a whole dime. This fired Danny up, and after telling Dave to get his own oil, Danny gathered his tools, and we headed back home.

When Dad got home from work, the old man drove down the lane to tell him what Danny had done and to grab the quart of oil. Dad, being tired from a long day at the foundry, did not appreciate how he tried to take advantage of Danny's help and sent him right back up the lane.

The next evening, after our dinner and chores, Linda and I got permission from Mom to go up to play with the girls since their parents were home. When we crossed the road, the old man came out of the house waving a rolled-up newspaper, screaming at us to leave. We outran him and circled the house to the back door. The mother, a slim, auburn-haired lady dressed in nice business clothes, heard the commotion and met us at the stairs. After first asking us where our shoes were, she invited us in as we explained why the old man was so angry. She quoted a few gospel verses and told us not to pay him any mind, then yelled for the girls.

The girls came down the stairs, and we tried to play kickball in the backyard, but we quickly noticed that it was too dangerous to play because of the busy street. Instead, we walked the grounds as they showed us everything on the property. A lady by the name of Mrs. Fox owned the property, and they rented from her. She very rarely stayed in the guest house, and it remained locked up. There was a large fishing pond in the back, and a tall chain-link fence surrounded it. Since the old man was so angry, we would probably never be able to fish there.

The girls' father had arrived home and appeared to have been drinking. We could hear him yelling with anger about their bicycles lying in the drive, and the girls had to go inside. We said goodbye to them and headed back home.

After crossing the street, we checked the mailbox, and our report cards had arrived. Running down the hill to the lane, we opened the envelopes with anticipation. We had all passed and would be moving on to the next grade level. Danny and Linda would be in the fifth grade, which was in a different school, but we would all still ride the same bus.

Danny had been held back in the third grade due to an eye injury and still needed more treatment later. I was going on to the fourth, and Vickie would be in the second. The other letter was a notice to register Roberta for the first grade in the fall. We ran home to give Mom the cards and tell her the news.

We would visit the girls a few more times. Pretending to be checking the mail, we would walk up the roadway and sneak up the small hill to get to their backyard to keep the old man from seeing us from the side window of the large house.

They invited us to attend Vacation Bible School at their church in the evenings for the whole week. We didn't really know what it was, but the girls assured us it would be fun. The whole idea of getting our baths, dressing in our school clothes, fixing our hair, and digging out our shoes from under the couch before six o'clock in the evening seemed ridiculous.

We did enjoy ourselves, and the small Baptist church was a beautiful place. We learned a little about the Bible, and they served us cookies and juice at break time. At craft time, Linda and I painted "praying hand" plaques in an antique bronze color and finished them with a gold glaze. The plaques were to be fired in the kiln and given to us on the last day of the bible school.

We snuck across the street from the old man on the last day, as we did each day for that week, but the girls' father was home early and had been drinking. We were instructed to sit quietly on the couch until they finished dinner, then we would leave for the church.

The family said some prayers over the meal and ate quietly without conversation. The father, a thin man in need of a shave and still wearing work clothes, ate like he was in a hurry. The silence in the room amplified the noises he made as he chewed his food, and I wished we just waited outside.

Then, after finishing her plate, the oldest girl reached across the table and picked up the last piece of fried chicken from the platter. The father, using his fork, stabbed her in the hand. With the other hand and a grunt, he took the piece of chicken from her. She let out a scream from the pain, and so did we as we watched the blood surface from the tines on the fork as it stuck up from her hand.

This was crazy. I jumped up from the couch to leave, and so did Linda.

Their father quickly turned his head toward us and yelled, "Sit back down!"

There was no way I was staying there, and I ran past the large wooden dining table in the room, still focused on her hand.

Linda followed me, and at the doorway, she turned and shouted, "You are going to go to hell. You are a devil!" That man and what he had done scared me, yet Linda confronted him and displayed no fear.

We ran down the stairs and out the door. We stopped running once we crossed the street and laughed, knowing that the drunken man couldn't catch us on a good day.

Sitting down at the top of the lane, we took our shoes and socks off. With them in hand, we discussed what had just happened as we walked down the lane; we decided not to tell Mom and Dad. Something was very wrong with that whole situation up there, and we felt sorry for the girls.

Arriving home, Mom asked, "Why aren't you two at bible school?"

Linda said quickly, "They must've left early, and we missed them," throwing our shoes under the couch.

I said nothing and followed Linda to the bedroom, where we changed into our play clothes.

She said to me, "Forget about it. Let's go fishing."

We took off outside, grabbed our poles, and met up with the others at the creek.

I knew we could not tell Mom the truth. She would never let us go back to that house, and who knows what Dad would say about that man hurting that girl. Besides, you could tell the girls feared their father, and maybe in the future, we could help them somehow.

We really didn't understand the whole church thing at that time, but we knew what happened at that dinner table wasn't right. We never said a prayer over our meal before we ate. Mom would make Dad's plate first from off the stove and freezer counter. Our food was never laid out on the table because there was never room. We bigger kids would make our own plates and eat while we helped the others cut their food.

Most of the time, Mom would eat while she cooked, and the smaller kids sat or stood in the five chairs left at the table, and we stood beside them. All the while, we were all constantly talking about the day and what needed to be done.

Ironically, I remember thinking about how we had spent a week making “praying hand” plaques, and that night, the oldest girl had a fork sticking out of her real hand in pain.

“Is that how Jesus felt?” I asked myself and wondered, *Should Linda and I have helped her get away from him?*

The girls were allowed to walk down the lane and deliver our plaques early the next day. The older girl apologized to their father and assured us her hand was fine under the white bandages, while the younger girl remained quiet. We would visit the girls sparingly throughout the summer but never when their father was home.

Chapter 5

Every Saturday morning, Dad would drive Mom to the grocery store early while we tended the children and watched the morning cartoons. As soon as the 1963 Ford Fairlane station wagon appeared at the curve in the lane, we ran out of the house to meet them, waiting impatiently for the car to stop. As soon as it did, Danny would flip down the back door to the station wagon so we could rummage through the many brown paper bags of groceries to find the white bag of mixed-up Brach's candies.

Surely, Linda found the bag and was the one who passed the candy out, dividing the candies up evenly and making sure the smaller kids didn't get a piece they would choke on. So, she kept all the extra for herself. Shoving our candies into our pockets, we helped unload the car and put the groceries away while the smaller children unwrapped and ate theirs, littering the front yard with wrappers.

Having put all the cold items away and doing a mental inventory of our favorites, Linda and I opened all the cereal boxes, removed the toys inside, and carefully closed them back up. I handed Linda the boxes and canned goods while she stood on the kitchen table and placed them in the high-wall cabinet. Linda would fold the many brown grocery bags and slide them next to the freezer while I put the "Top Value" stamps in the saving books. I would give Mom the total count so she knew how many more she needed to save to get something from the catalog. After that, we collected our cereal toys and headed outside to play with the others until Mom told us what to do next.

Uncle Buggy, Mom's oldest brother, was a huge man and constantly chewed tobacco. He spoke in a deep, calm voice yet laughed with a playful chuckle. Mom told us he would be dropping Grandma and Grandpa off later today from Hazard, and we had a lot of extra chores to do. We had to make up extra places for them to sleep, break green beans and get them on the stove for dinner, clean the house, and pick up all those candy papers strewn in the yard. We all had something to do.

Grandpa would start on the much-needed room addition to the house, and Grandma would help Mom with us kids for a couple of weeks. Linda and I finished up with the animals and put new strings on our fishing poles while we waited for them to arrive. We would be in need of some bait and decided on worms rather than crawdads since our day would be short. We had spent about half the afternoon unstacking the concrete blocks to get to the damp enough ground to dig up a tin can full of worms for bait. Grandma loved to fish, and as soon as she arrived, we would be ready to show her our newest fishing spot.

Linda and I were going to take her downstream to the big hole. We had been fishing a lot since school let out, and the water there was deep. Rather than following the creek all the way down to it, Grandma could walk the trails we had made through the woods, past the burnt trash hole, and only have to cross the creek once.

They arrived late afternoon. As soon as they settled in and after dinner and chores, Dad and Grandpa were measuring for the house addition, and Grandma headed toward the creek with us.

Danny, Linda, Vickie, Roberta, and I walked up the lane with Grandma, telling her about school and this new spot to fish. At the curve, we followed our footpath through a stretch of woods to a small streambed that only had water when it rained from the mountain runoff. We followed the streambed down to the creek's edge and grabbed a quick drink of water from another pipe we had shoved into the clay bank, tapping into the spring, and crossed to the other side.

Rounding the bend in the creek, we passed a long, sandy, shallow spot and some rough rapids. The creek had cut into the farm field, leaving a very steep clay bank on the opposite side and a sandy spot for us to fish from. A large rock bed rested in behind here to a tree line where a tractor road led into more farm fields.

Linda had swum in the test how deep the fishing hole was and could not touch the bottom a few weeks earlier. Since I wore glasses, I swam close to the bank or a little downstream where it was shallower, and the creek narrowed before getting rough again. Linda and I had explored as far down as possible until we approached a small white house close to the creek bank and turned around.

Danny, Vickie, and Roberta swam in the shallow spot while Grandma, Linda, and I fished. After catching a few small bluegill and sunfish and throwing them back, we headed home before dark.

The following day, I woke to the smell of coffee and bacon frying. After dressing for the day and putting up the rollaway bed, I rushed out to gather the eggs and feed the chickens. With pinned-up excitement and anticipation, I ate breakfast and rushed out to dig up more worms. We were going fishing all day with Grandma while Dad and the others built the foundation for the room addition.

Dad and Mom's good friends, Vernon, a short, round man with a weathered face, and his wife, Sarah "Tootie," arrived early to help. Tootie didn't care much about fishing any farther downstream than the spot at our footpath and stayed back with Roberta, who was six and a half years old, to take care of Billy Joe and feed the men, allowing Mom to go with us. Grandma, with a few beers in a bag and a transistor radio, tuned to the Cincinnati Reds' ball game. Mom and the rest of us took off to the new fishing hole.

Resembling a small parade, we arrived at the spot without incident. The water was as calm as glass, and the sun was just beginning to get hot. The fish were biting pretty well. Grandma, Mom, Linda, and I fished while the others played on the rocks and in the sand nearby. After a while, we decided to swim downstream, a short distance away. Vickie, Kay, and Bam sat close to the bank, cooling David off while Linda scooped tiny dollar-sized turtles out of the sand at the water's edge. Danny, Reva, and I were swimming in the chest-deep water when we noticed the water start changing to a muddy brown color. Then Danny looked up with a puzzled expression.

"What's that?" he said, "do you hear it?"

It sounded like a train in the far distance but different. Then, at the same time, we looked upstream at the first bend. Suddenly, a huge wall of muddy water and debris appeared, roaring around the bend and coming right at us!

With loud screams to hurry and run, we all took off down the creek bank toward the house Linda and I had seen a few weeks ago. Linda and I shouted instructions to the others as we all raced on the rocks from the huge wall of water and debris. Near the house, we found a place to cross the creek. Once across, Danny spotted a footpath leading up the bank.

Danny yelled, “Follow me. Hurry!” as he made his way up the bank.

Behind him, Vickie, with little David on her hip, dragging Bam by the hand, was having trouble getting up the bank. The path was slick from the water off their clothes, so she passed David to Danny, and Linda helped push them up.

The water was rising at this time, and Linda grabbed Kay and slung her up the path to Danny, ripping her clean out of her shirt. I was at the bottom of the path, holding Reva’s hand and a small tree as the wall of water and logs struck us. Fighting to keep from being knocked down and Reva’s body twisting in the water as I held tight to her hand, Linda came in to help us claw our way up the bank.

Once out of harm’s way, we realized that three of us were missing. Mom, Grandma, and Donna, who was only two years old at the time. In a panic, we all ran toward the house. At the same time, a short, red-haired lady came out of the house yelling at her two boys, whom she assumed were fighting again from the screaming outside. She stopped when she saw our platoon rushing at her.

“What’s going on out here? Where did all these kids come from? Who are they? Oh my! The water!”

The flash flood was terrible enough, but she scared us to death. After quickly explaining who we were and what had happened, we all ran back home through the cornfields, crying and scared that our mom, Grandma, and Donna had washed away. We stopped atop the fishing hole and looked over the steep bank. The brown, muddy flood water stretched from bank to bank, and there was no sign of them. They were gone, washed away.

We made it home, still crying and hysterical, all of us talking at once, telling Dad and Grandpa what had happened. Grandpa's knees buckled in disbelief, and he sank onto a cement block as Dad and Vernon ran to the old 1947 Chevrolet pickup truck and drove off. Slowing down at the curve, Vernon pointed to the flood water in the creek road, and Dad sped off.

Tootie, hugging us, somehow managed to calm us all down with a sympathetic ear as we explained what happened to her and Roberta. Eating the peanut butter and jelly sandwiches Tootie made for us, we waited outside for Dad and Vernon to return. Finally, the truck came around the curve carrying some passengers in the cargo bed. Mom! Grandma! Donna! Thank God!

They had seen the water coming and knew they could not outrun it, so they ran across the large rock bed to the farm fields behind the fishing hole. Following a tractor road along many acres of fields, they managed to walk up to the street where Dad found and picked them up. Our family was all together and safe.

Chapter 6

The flood water filled the creek road, and it took days to lower and clear up before we could swim and fish again. We spent the next few days watching Grandpa build the foundation and playing with the newly hatched chickens. We built a small closed pen so they could be protected from raccoons or foxes until they grew big enough for the larger pen and chicken coop.

Grandma showed us how to clip the wings of the younger chickens that wanted to fly over the fence. We were constantly catching these young chickens and putting them back into the pen when they flew out. One by one, we clipped only one of their wings using a large pair of scissors and laughed when they tried to fly. They were able, however, to just get off the ground, make a complete circle, and remain in the pen. We would be rotating chickens out at the end of summer, so we had to make sure nothing got the young ones.

Grandpa had finished the foundation by the end of the week, and Dad, Vernon, and Danny were going to help him work on a slab of concrete in front of the house for a future porch. Mom told us to grab the children and head out. We were told to find something to do so we were not in their way.

The creek was still too rough for the smaller children. Since it had rained a few days earlier, the runoff stream had a good, steady flow of water. So we grabbed a pail and headed up through the woods to the stream. Using the pail to scoop water, we carried it to the top of our path and poured it down, creating a soupy mess of mud. One by one, we took turns sliding down the hill. The smaller kids went the farthest and rolled in the mud at the bottom, trying to keep their footing. With a quick rinse-off in the stream and a refill of the pail, we spent the entire day laughing and playing in the mud.

Hours later, Mom, Grandma, and Tootie walked up to the trails and watched what Linda had us doing. They laughed as we all took turns showing off. Rinsing most of the mud out of our hair and off ourselves in the stream, we headed home for dinner. Mom would not let us in the house, of course, and Dad, Vernon, and Grandpa laughed at the sight of us. We had ruined our clothes, tattered them, and had holes worn through them from the fun of the day. We were merely adorning rags. We all had to strip down to bare skin. Grandma sprayed us with a garden hose as we all stood in the front yard, washing the mud out of our hair and ears.

Earlier, while in the woods, Grandma had spotted a large patch of catnip in the trails and took some home to show us how to make tea with it. After dinner, we all had some, but I didn't care much for the taste of it. Other than that, it was an uneventful night, and with the help of the tea, we were all in bed early.

The next day, the creek had finally gone down, and the ground dried enough to sit on the bank to fish. The creek road was filled with large rocks and mud and would require some grading before it could be used again by vehicles.

The flood had changed the creek some and washed that big rock out of our swimming hole, sending it further downstream. The high water had cut into the bank down from that spot, leaving a large gray clay shelf. This would be a good place to spend the days molding ashtrays and painting ourselves while watching the others swim.

We were able to fish a few more times before Grandma and Grandpa had to head back to Hazard. Analyzing the creek after the flood, we noticed only a few rock bass now ran in the channel, and the crawdads were hard to find except in the deep water.

Most of the swallows were gone, and the few that remained were trying to bore new holes into the newly eroded creek bank. The pipe for our spring water was still in place, but we had to replace the drinking cup that we kept hanging from it.

We went downstream and fished the big fishing hole with Grandma a few times, and the red-haired boys, Timmy and Jimmy, could hear us playing there.

They would walk over through the cornfield and talk to us from atop the big bank. We had seen the boys on the school bus and didn't know they were our neighbors until the flood, and we climbed the bank near their house. Grandma got a kick out of the boys and, a few years later, started calling this spot “Phillips’ Fishing Hole.”

The flood had cut a large part of their property away, and the side door of their house was very close to the edge of the bank. The footpath that we had climbed up to save ourselves the day of the flood was missing.

Danny talked to Dad about helping them fix the bank since he had access to a bulldozer. Dad agreed to go down and see what he could do but had to wait a few more days or even weeks for the water to recede and the banks to dry out more.

At the end of the week, it was time for Grandma and Grandpa to head back, and Uncle Buggy showed up early in the morning to pick them up. Danny went back with them to spend the summer and help them out. He could fix whatever machinery was broken and was able to drive anything that had wheels. We would be going down for vacation in early August, and he could ride back with us. We gave Grandma our "praying hand" plaques from the bible school and waved goodbye as they drove off down the lane.

Timmy and Jimmy swam and fished with us often at the fishing hole that summer. Mom had to explain to us older girls that it was not proper to swim without our shirts when the boys were around, and we had to start packing around a towel. Vickie and I did not like swimming with the younger boy, Timmy. At times, he stood on our backs while we were underwater and held us down. I think it was his way of flirting. All it did, though, was get him beat up.

Dad eventually made it down to their house with the bulldozer and repaired the creek bank by smashing and stacking a few old cars, laying them on top of each other, and filling the cavities with gravel.

Dad knew their father since they worked together at the foundry. They had four other children, two girls and two more boys, who were much older than us. All the boys helped Dad with the backfilling, and the girls helped their mother in the kitchen with food for when the job was finished.

Touring the house, Linda and I saw a drinking bar in one room. A display of liquor bottles and fancy drinking glasses adorned the shelves, along with neon beer signs. The dimly lit room smelled of cigarette smoke, and knowing this was an adult gathering place, we shuffled past the room quickly. We noticed an operating telephone hanging on the wall that we could possibly use in case of emergencies since we did not have one. We had been using Dave Hall's telephone, but he was still angry at us about the lawn mower incident. This house was a little farther away, but they weren't mad at us.

Chapter 7

We headed upstream many times during the next few weeks, whenever it did not rain, and spent the whole day there with all the kids except Donna, David, and Billy Joe so Mom could get things done. She thought they were just too small for us to keep an eye on all day while at the creek. Linda supervised while the rest of us teamed up; I watched over Reva, Vickie took care of Bam, and Roberta kept track of Kay as we made our way up to Walter's Pond.

We played all over the grove of vines and examined the piles of junk but never found much of anything we could use. The smaller kids tired out easily, of course, and after a few trips of carrying them back home, we had to find an easier route. We made a path up the bank near the spring to get to the farm field. There, we walked the edge of the field until we hit the farmer's tractor road. The field seemed never-ending to us, but as long as we ate our sandwiches up there, we made it back just fine on our own two legs.

Almost daily, Linda and I tried to catch the huge carp that was trapped at the turtle pond due to the flash flood while the others stacked rocks and caught toads. One day, as I sat on a large rock studying my line, Linda sneaked up behind me and threw a huge black and yellow garden spider into my long hair.

"Black Widow. You are going to die!" she yelled.

Terrified, I swatted at my hair and sensed it crawling on my head, ready to bite. I threw my pole down, jumped up, and ran, following the other end of the tractor road leading to the junk piles and toward his farm. I climbed over a fence and cut through the cornfield, running through the rows of tall field corn, the leaves slicing my face, arms, and legs, and headed straight to the house as fast as I could. I then climbed over the fence and barbed wire next to the house and ran inside, crying and screaming for Mom to find the spider.

In disbelief at my cut-up body, she ran a bath for me and helped wash my hair. While gripping my chin and combing out my tangles, she kept showing me the comb to assure me there was no spider. She made a sandwich for me and told me to lie down and take a nap.

She said, “There aren’t any black widows around here. Linda is just being Linda. She's just flat-out being mean.”

I felt that spider in my hair for about a week afterward, and Linda never got in trouble for it either. I would just have to find a way to pay her back.

A few days later, it was the Fourth of July. Mom’s relatives and Dad’s friends would be stopping in to visit. It was a nice hot summer day full of swimming, fishing, horseshoes, grilling out, and later, fireworks, sparklers, and music.

Mom’s sister, Anna (we called her “Aunt Duck”), her husband, Orb, and their two children, Amy and Tommy, stopped in. Uncle Buggy, his wife, Laura, and their daughter, Rose Marie, arrived a little later. We enjoyed playing with the city kids and watching them get their nice clothes dirty. Aunt Duck never cared since her daughter, Amy, a few years older than us, was a tomboy, too. Aunt Laura was different and a true city lady. She called us demons and would always preach the gospel to us when Mom and Dad were not around. We were not demons, of course. We knew how to act politely when we were expected to, but I sadly admit we did enjoy aggravating her.

The ladies had spent the day preparing dinner while the men fried chicken and cooked burgers and hot dogs on the grill. We spent the hot day playing outside, and when they yelled for us at dinnertime, we came up from the creek to eat.

The older kids helped to carry the food to the picnic table. Linda was carrying a large glass bowl of potato salad when she tripped on one of Billy Joe's blankets that lay in the yard. The bowl shattered on the hard ground, and she fell right on top of it, slicing her leg wide open.

Aunt Duck heard the commotion and yelled, "Phyllis! Linda has cut her leg!"

Mom hated the sight of blood and never even looked while yelling for Dad to help. From the grill across the yard, he ran to Linda and scooped her up as blood gushed from her leg. He rushed her into the house to the kitchen, threw everything out of the sink, and turned the water on to clean it and see how bad it was. It was not a deep cut, but it was about ten inches long from just below her knee, almost to her ankle. He stopped the bleeding and put that red stuff on it, Merthiolate, while blowing on it to ease the burn as Linda gritted her teeth. He then taped the cut shut and wrapped it to keep the dirt out.

Linda would be down for a few days, and who knew how long it would be before she could get in the water to swim? I was going to enjoy putting that red stuff on her leg after what she did to me with the spider but I knew that big cut would not slow us down any.

We all ate our dinner, and Vickie and I helped clean the dishes and put food away as Linda sat in a lawn chair and watched. Uncle Buggy and his family headed home as some of Dad's friends started stopping in. Vernon and Tootie, Gray (Dad's best friend from the Army), and his wife Wilma all brought fireworks, and we could hardly sit still waiting for dark. Three more couples and their friends stopped in; they were strangers to us kids, but they seemed very friendly. The men pitched horseshoes and drank beer while the women passed Billy Joe around, and we kids went about our business playing until dark.

Mom took Billy Joe to bed while Tootie and Linda passed out sparklers to all of us. Carefully lighting each one, we ran in circles, chasing each other in the yard and enjoying the lights. Collecting the metal wands as they went out so no one would lose an eye, Tootie would light another until they were all gone. The men had since placed the firework cones in the driveway to be lit, and we all lined up on the grass to watch in front of the ladies. One by one, we watched the beautiful spray of lights drop from the sky, followed by the loud booms. This seemed to have lasted forever until Dad started playing the guitar as we all gathered around and listened.

Dad, whose professional name was Bill "Zeke," played the guitar and just about every kind of musical instrument quite well. He played the Nashville circuit before recording a few records with his band, The Rhythm Rascals, in the late 50s to early 60s and played locally up until about 1967. One of his songs, "I'll Pay You Back", was number one on the Rockabilly music charts in

1959. At this time, he met and married Mom. After having throat surgery, he stopped recording and focused on raising a large family, but he never stopped playing music for all of us.

Some of Dad's friends had already left, and Aunt Duck and her family just pulled out of the lane. Noticing a few of the smaller kids had fallen asleep on a blanket outside, Vickie and I carried Donna and David into the house for bedtime. We were on our way back outside to get Kay and Bam when we noticed Roberta was missing. She was not in bed and was not outside with the rest of us, so we told Mom. In a complete panic, we all went on a search. Vernon and Tootie drove up the drive to Dave Hall's house to call the police. An officer arrived in a short while and joined the search.

Linda limped around, helping us as we checked the cars, the outbuildings, and the chicken coop. Dad spoke to the policeman, giving the names of those who left in case she had crawled into one of their cars and gone to sleep. Dad suggested she may have left with Uncle Buggy since she enjoyed playing with Rose Marie, and he would bring her home the next day, but without a phone, we could not verify. Mom argued with him, saying that did not happen, and continued searching as we all did.

The policeman was completely confused with all the children running around and kept asking, "Is this one the one you are looking for?" as he pointed at each of us at random.

"NO! We are looking for Berta!" Mom yelled as she went inside to search the house again.

After looking under the beds, behind the couch and coal stove, and throwing out the many coats from the bottom of the small closet in their bedroom, she finally opened the cabinet doors to the kitchen sink. It was there Roberta lay curled in a ball, fast asleep. Unaware of the panic she caused, Mom picked her up and put her into bed. We found out later that she had become afraid of one of Dad's friends and the noise of the fireworks, so she crawled into the cabinet and fell asleep.

Afterward, we all went back outside and waved goodbye to the policeman. We laughed about the big scare but were relieved nothing bad had happened to her. Dad played music well into the night, and we all slowly made our way to bed as we got tired.

Chapter 8

After doing our routine chores, Linda and the rest of us went down to the creek so Mom could mop the floors and not have us in the way. We even had the smaller kids with us and were entertaining them in the sand along the creek bank and swimming where it was safe. After a short while, a pale-skinned man in his late thirties walked up carrying a fancy fishing pole, a bucket with some bottled beers, and a little Styrofoam container with store-bought worms. He took out the beers and sat them on the bank along with the bait and turned the bucket over to sit down.

"Is this a good spot to fish?" he asked.

I shied away from speaking to him, but Linda, sitting on the bank watching us and fishing a short distance away, replied, "Not too bad today." The cut on her leg was still in a bandage, so she was not able to swim.

I recognized the man from the Fourth of July party a few days earlier. He had come down with one of the couples that Dad knew.

He said, "I asked your mom if I could come down and fish. She said I could. She told me you girls were down here playing and fishing."

I watched as Linda talked, and he baited his hook. After he cast the line in, he pulled out his knife to open his beer. They sat fishing and talking a bit while we all continued playing. Then, when his bottle was empty, he threw it high into the air behind him. The bottle busted as it hit the rocks, and the sound startled us. I was angry, looking over at the brown broken glass on the rocks, and got out of the water to pick it up. We were told never to break bottles down there since I almost cut one of my toes off a couple of summers back. Linda was angry, too.

"What are you doing? Don't bust the bottles!" she told him. "We all aren't wearing shoes, and we don't want to cut ourselves on that glass. Look! That's what happened to my leg!" she said, as she pointed to the bandage.

The man shrugged his shoulders and said something to her as I walked over and started to pick up the glass. He opened another beer, reeled the line in on his pole, and laid his pole down on the bank. He stood up and stretched and then walked over to where the rest of the children were playing.

"Who wants me to pick them up and throw them into the water? It'll be fun," he said as he waded into the water.

I looked over at Linda, and she had a questionable expression on her face yet nodded as if to permit them.

Pushing his beer bottle into the back of his shorts, he reached over and grabbed Reva, lifting her up and tossing her into the water. She came up laughing, and then he grabbed Bam, four and a half years old, and threw her. By then, Kay, three and a half, was in line. Kay could not swim well, but we taught her how to float and kick like a tadpole. It all seemed to be in good fun for a while, until he threw his empty beer bottle at the bank, and it broke right at the water's edge where the others were playing. Vickie and Roberta picked Donna and David up and moved them away from the glass so they would not get cut, and Linda yelled at him again.

"Don't do that!"

"It was an accident," he said, smiling. "I tried to throw it on the sand. I didn't think it would break." He continued throwing the girls into the water.

I went over to pick up the glass. He then picked up Roberta, and it seemed as if he deliberately threw her head first into the shallow part close to the bank. With her face red and scraped from the rocks, she came over to me for inspection.

"You're okay," I said as I ran my hand across her head, checking for blood. The expression on Linda's face showed a sense of anger and fear, and I knew this man was trouble.

Picking up the shards of broken glass, I whispered to Roberta, "Run up and get Mom. Fast!"

He threw the others a few more times, and then he picked up Donna, who was just two and a half years old, to throw her.

Linda dropped her pole, jumped up, and yelled, "She can't swim!"

He looked at Linda, smiled, and threw Donna anyway. Vickie swam in to get her as she struggled to keep her head above water. Linda grabbed and held on to David as Roberta and Mom were coming up the creek bank. She held in her hand what looked like a wadded-up towel.

"What do you think you're doing?" Mom yelled. "Get away from my kids! I suggest you leave! Now!" Her hand shook from under the towel as she pointed her Colt 38 Special pistol at him from a short distance and tried not to scare the others.

He saw the gun and raised his hands slightly as he waded out of the water and walked toward his things.

"I didn't do anything wrong. This is all a misunderstanding," he said as he grabbed his fishing pole and took off walking across the creek bank.

Mom told us all to stay back as she followed him up the footpath to his car. She was still pointing the gun at him as he got in and drove out of the lane. Then she came back and told us never to swim with anyone like that again. Mom told us that if we saw any more strangers at the creek, we were to run home and tell her immediately.

We went about our day, and when Dad got home from work, Mom told him what had happened. Dad told her that if he came back, do not even give him a chance to get out of the car; just start shooting! He was very angry and was going to talk to his friends and find out who the man was.

About a week had passed, and we were all playing ball in the yard and dragging each other around in our homemade wagons up to the "three trees" and back. It had rained the past two days, and since the flash flood, we learned to stay away from the creek for a while just in case it flooded again. Then, a car came down the lane, pulled up into the yard just past the picnic table, and parked just shy of the "three trees". One of the girls pointed to the car and said, "That guy in the car is back."

The same man from the creek got out and started waxing his car in the yard.

He smiled and asked, "Do one of you want to help? I'll pay you."

We all stood, frozen, looking at the man from a distance.

Meanwhile, Linda recognized the car and went inside to tell Mom, who came out of the house and walked across the yard, pointing the gun at him.

"I told you never to come back!" she shouted. "This isn't no car wash! Get out of here!"

He acted surprised but stood still and told her to calm down.

"I am calm! Now leave!" she screamed. A few seconds passed, and the man did not move. Mom shut her eyes and fired the gun at him.

The bullet hit his car, and he jumped. We watched as he wrestled with the door handle, finally opened it, and scrambled in. As he was trying to start the engine, Mom fired again, hitting the hubcap. He backed the car up and was putting it in gear when she closed her eyes and fired again, again, and again until the gun made a silent click. He was gone. The car had six bullet holes in it as it sped off. Mom's face then displayed a sense of calm.

"Doubt he'll be back!" she said, grabbing David from the wagon before heading to the house.

Chapter 9

It started raining late that evening and was still raining the next morning when we all woke up. Trudging out to feed the animals and collect the eggs in the rainy mess was a challenge. With the foundation for the room addition outside the side door, we had to go in and out the front. Mom put a washtub of water out on the porch for us to dip our feet and clean them off so we would not track the mud inside. Using the bottom part of our shirt as an egg basket, we nearly broke the eggs when our wet feet slipped on the tile floor.

We had already eaten breakfast, and the others were tired of playing school from the day before. Vickie took up the much-needed ironing while Mom got the rest of the kids somehow interested in the "Uncle Al" television show and sat down to rock Billy Joe.

Waiting for the rain to stop, Linda and I grabbed some crayons and coloring books and sneaked into Mom and Dad's closet to color. Needing a light, we took a small lamp from the top of their chest and plugged it in. We sat for over an hour on top of a stack of coats that lay at the bottom of the closet, coloring and waiting for the rain to stop.

I thought to myself, *Peace and quiet, finally,* as I heard the others outside in the other room. Peace and quiet around Linda was always short-lived, however.

Bored with coloring, Linda said to me, "What would happen if you were to spit on this light bulb?"

"I don't know," I said as I glanced at the hot, brightly lit bulb. "I never really thought about it. It would probably just sizzle, you think?"

That being said, she spits.

Pop! The light goes out, and we are splattered with hot glass.

Throwing down our crayons and books, we jump up, banging into each other in the pitch darkness, beating and clawing at the door to find the door knob. It opens and we fly out onto the floor. Mom, of course, comes running into the room, holding Billy Joe.

"What is going on?"

"The bulb busted," Linda said. "Look at all the glass, it burned us!" brushing at her arms and legs.

After checking us over, Mom said, "You all are alright, just don't pick at the marks. Now get outside. It quit raining. I'll clean this up."

I said nothing as Linda looked at me with a smirk, and we both took off outside.

"The bulb will bust and burn you," she said with a silent snicker. She grabbed a ball on the front porch and took off across the yard. "Come on, catch!"

We threw the ball back and forth for a while and then decided to explore the wood trails to see how much water was in the streambed. I had a few blisters on my arms from the light bulb, but I forgot about them once we started playing. Walking through the trails with the mud squishing through our toes and collecting on our feet, we went to the streambed to wash off. This was a mess; it needed to dry up some before we could play here. Linda and I picked a small bundle of catnip and headed home to make a batch of tea, as Grandma had shown us.

The others were playing ball in the yard, and Mom was out back doing laundry. I washed the catnip while Linda dug out the large kettle from under the sacks of potatoes and filled it halfway with water. Throwing the sprigs in and turning on the stove, we sat at the table and waited for the water to boil. Reva came inside and asked Linda to climb the fence to get the ball they had kicked over. They were too small to clear the barbed wire on top.

"Get Vickie or Berta to get it," Linda said.

"They are out back helping Mom wash clothes," she said.

Getting the ball was a whole lot easier than doing laundry, so Linda and I went to get the ball. After playing a few innings of kickball with the kids, we heard Mom from inside the house screaming, "Linda!" She opened the front door, and a cloud of smoke came billowing out.

I looked at Linda and yelled, "The tea!" and we took off running to the house.

The water had boiled out, and the greens had started to burn. The white cabinets, walls, and ceiling were black from the smoke, and the foul smell almost knocked us out.

"I've had about enough of you two today," Mom said. "You damn near burnt the house down! Now get a rag and start cleaning this up before your Daddy gets home!"

And that we did. It took us hours, and the lecture on "not to leave the stove while you're cooking" is still in my head today.

Chapter 10

Mom had spent many afternoons sewing A-lined dresses for the girls while we all went swimming and playing in the creek. Using the treadle sewing machine (I believe we all sewed our fingers in it at least once until she finally gave it to Grandma) and a pink and blue gingham material, she made dresses that tied at the shoulders so they fit all of the smaller children from Reva on down. She had been buying shorts and matching shirts for us older children and David each week for our vacation trip to Hazard to visit Grandma and Grandpa and to pick up Danny.

The night before our trip, we took our baths and put on our new clothes to sleep in to avoid the morning rush. We had to move the couch out to find our shoes, which had not seen daylight since school let out. It was difficult to sleep due to the excitement, and we woke up easily.

Still dark outside, Linda, Vickie, Roberta, and I helped carry the other sleeping children to the station wagon. With the luggage strapped to the top, we headed out. By the time we arrived at the first toll booth on the Mountain Parkway, the other children started waking up. We stopped at a roadside pull-off to use the bathroom, stretch our legs, and eat quickly before hitting the curvy mountain roads.

We left the highway and drove through town and the winding roads to the holler road. Pulling into the dirt road just past the row of many mailboxes, I noticed the large swinging bridge was still there. If the creek was high, the bridge was used to get to the other side, and your vehicle had to be left. Almost everyone drove large trucks and was able to drive on through. The small creek was very low, yet the water ran crystal clear over the large, flat, orange-colored rocks.

The road looked dry and barren from the lack of rain, and orange dust collected onto the car windows. We drove past the family cemetery on the hill and pulled up to the first house, a dark gray, weathered wood home with a rusty tin roof, and parked next to a pile of coal. Danny jumped down from the porch, filled with rocking chairs, to greet us as we all spilled out of the car.

Our great Grandma (we called her Redheaded Grandma) lived here with Aunt Lizzy, Uncle Dewey, and our cousins Et and Beckum. Aunt Lizzy snatched the baby, Billy Joe, immediately from Mom at the car while the others greeted us with hugs and clarifications as to what all of our names were.

Throwing our shoes in the back of the station wagon, we went inside to get a drink of fresh, cold water out of a large polished steel pail. Many times a day, Beckum took the empty pail to the spring at the top of the mountain to fill it. The water was the coldest I had ever tasted. We enjoyed playing with Beckum, an overgrown kid who was always running around and could spit tobacco clear across the old porch and hit the pail every time. He was up in the years of age but acted somewhat like a small boy, someone we could relate to.

We really did not know the others very well because they did not visit often, so Danny took Linda, Vickie, Roberta, and me up the holler road to Grandma and Grandpa's house. The rest stayed back to visit for a while before driving there.

The red dirt felt like soft powder on our feet as the road was dry and tire-marked due to the lack of rain. We stopped and petted the old mule, whose fence sat close to the road, before continuing on up a slight hill at the base of the mountain and a few more "S" turns toward Grandma's.

The trees towered above us as they grew from the mountain, and if it wasn't for the small creek and foothills on the opposite side of the road, they would probably block the sky. Danny knew everyone here and had a story to tell us about each one as we passed the few homes resting in the narrow valley. It seemed as if we had walked for miles before finally arriving at Grandma's.

Grandma and Grandpa yelled "hello" to us in their Southern accent from the porch of the white house, which sat high in the mountain. We crossed a footbridge made of two oak trees, bound together with chains, which rested on the opposing banks of the small creek underneath. There was no bridge for cars, so everything had to be carried over the footbridge and up a long, narrow, winding path to the house.

A large, long set of steps led up to the high porch with the railings and gate painted a bright blue. The house rested on tall horizontal logs resembling stilts in front, and the mountain was cut out for the house in the back. An outhouse sat close to a stack of coal near the back porch, and a garden grew just past a small front yard. A chicken pen and coop, a pig pen, and a smokehouse rested in the back, chiseled into the mountainside.

A bench swing and rocking chairs lined the front porch. Two old coffee cans sat near the railing, which smoldered smoke to keep bugs away. Inside, Grandpa's recliner sat next to the coal stove, and a small table held his pipe and tobacco. A black leather couch and a console TV filled the room, and our "praying hand" plagues hung from the cream-colored wall near the door to the porch.

A faint smell of burnt coal was apparent. The floors creaked under the linoleum throughout the house, and beds filled the other rooms. A large, gold pocket watch-style clock hung from the wall next to the refrigerator, and a large pot of green beans and potatoes was cooking on the stove.

We went outside and sat on the swing and rocking chairs on the porch and talked about the fishing hole and the redheaded boys downstream and how Linda cut her leg, which was finally healed. After a while, we spotted the station wagon approaching and ran down to help unload and get the smaller children up to the house.

Grandma laughed at how we resembled a small army of ants packing our things up to the house along the winding path from her porch view. Mom came in and immediately put Billy Joe on a bed to sleep. Then, more of Mom's relatives began showing up.

Uncle Aaron and Elsie stopped in. They were recently engaged, and from what I remember, Grandma was not happy about it for some reason. Aaron was Mom's youngest brother, and he started telling jokes and stories while Elsie helped in the kitchen with dinner.

Aunt Murry and C.B., with their children, arrived close to dinnertime. They all sat at the table, talking and joking while we sat on the living room floor, eating and listening.

Linda and I went with Danny to feed the hogs and chickens after dinner while the others cleaned up the dishes. A few of the kids went home with Murry and C.B. for the night, and we sat on the porch until bedtime was announced. It was eight o'clock, still daylight!

Tired from the long day, however, we went to bed without too much complaint.

Chapter 11

We woke up early to the smell of coffee, bacon frying, clattering of dishes, and baking pans. I noticed it was five o'clock in the morning; no wonder bedtime was at eight in the evening. The rooster was crowing, and the sun was starting to come up when some of us sat down to eat. It seemed as if we weren't in a hurry down here. Grandma, Grandpa, and Dad sat around talking and drinking coffee for hours until the fog lifted from between the mountains. We woke the others to eat, finish the dishes, and find something to do.

Danny, Linda, and I decided to run the holler road down to Redheaded Grandma's house and visit them for a while until lunchtime. We messed with the mule again. Linda and I waded the creek a bit to cool off, and Danny told us to get out of it. He didn't know why, except for snakes, so we headed back.

We ate lunch and played in the yard with the others. We played under the house to escape the hot sun and watched the hogs in their shady pen. Murry, C.B., and the kids stopped in and brought some of their toys to entertain the others.

After dinner, they headed out, and we cleaned up and got ready for the next day while Dad and Mom rode into town to get milk and diapers at "The Goose." It was the local marketplace, and Grandpa and Aaron had recently helped restore it. The top of the store was shaped like a goose, and the actual store was in its body. (As time passed, the marketplace eventually closed, and the building was restored into an inn.)

After doing the breakfast dishes and hanging some laundry, Linda and I noticed Grandma kept walking out to the smokehouse. We snuck out and caught her drinking beer she had gotten from Dad. Hazard being a dry town, Grandma was glad Dad had stopped at the "Last Chance" store on the way in. He purchased beer, and she hid it from Grandpa in the smokehouse. She told us to keep it a secret, but we noticed she might be a little drunk. We hid her three empty cans and sat her down in the yard to play with the other kids until we could get her some coffee to straighten her up. She was funny when she drank and tended to act like us kids, so at the time, I never understood why she wasn't allowed to. This would be the first of many times when Linda and I were asked to sneak beers for her and hide them from Grandpa and Mom.

We would run the holler road and visit our Redheaded Grandma and the others the next few days and keep an eye on Grandma. Linda and I went to the creek to swim and look for crawdads one day. Mom panicked and told us to get out of it. I remember her saying we would get snakebit, and the coal miners may have messed with the water. Without the creek, we really didn't have much to do here, and it was too hot not to be able to play in it. Mom said we would be leaving in the morning, and I knew I would miss Grandma and Grandpa and the others, but it would be nice to get back home.

We piled in the car the next morning for the long drive home the same way as the way down, except we made room for Danny. We stopped at the Natural Bridge Park on the way back. We played while Dad grilled, and Mom made us lunch. After eating, we got back onto the Parkway and drove on.

Chapter 12

It had not rained in weeks, and everything looked wilted from the heat. We had just got back from Hazard and had a lot to do before school started again.

The days were hot, so Linda and I had gotten up early and built a fire for the washtub we needed to process the non-laying hens. We had to rotate them and get them ready for the freezer since they had stopped producing eggs. We spent the morning plucking the feathers from the older chickens while the other children ran around the yard playing with the chicken feet. It was funny watching them chase each other as they pulled the tendons, making the foot appear to be alive.

Dad's friends would be stopping to visit. They would be spending the whole day talking, drinking beers, and pitching horseshoes. Linda and I were excited for the chance to make some money selling sweet corn for twenty-five cents a dozen to Gray and Wilma and Vernon and Tootie. We would give Mom the money to pay for the layaway we had at the local department store, Woolco, or order the school clothes we picked from Alden's fall catalog. The garden was coming in fast, and we had to start canning soon.

Tootie helped Mom in getting the fresh chickens ready to freeze and cut a few to fry on the outside grill. Vickie and Roberta broke the freshly picked green beans from the garden and cut potatoes for the salad. Linda and I were busy picking thirty dozen ears of corn, twelve ears at a time, laying an extra ear on the ground to avoid losing count. We shoved them into the brown grocery bags and lugged them out to the edge of the field. At the other end of the garden, men were busy picking tomatoes, peppers, and cucumbers since everything was getting ripe simultaneously.

The other children played outside all day and were filthy from the dust in the yard. Gray had also emptied his pockets of change and threw it out into the dusty driveway for us to try and find. He did that every time he came to visit.

Since Linda and I were itchy from the cornfield, we took the children to the creek for a quick rinse-off before dinner. We convinced Gray to walk with us down to see the creek and our "horse tree". The tree was washed up to the end of our footpath during the flash flood in June. The strong branches jetted out from the trunk and were viewed snow-white from the sun. The huge root ball kept the tree nice and stable as it rested on a sandbar.

As Linda's wound was healing, we made small saddles on the branches. We had wrapped an old rag for a horn, using hay string for stirrups tied to a large nail, and made it easy to get up and ride. This was a much nicer place for the tree, comparatively. Even if we lost our balance, we would fall onto the soft sandbar. It allowed the smaller kids to play there more often. After being there for a while, we went down to swim. Gray asked us about catching turtles there. Linda could catch them in the sandy spots along the water's edge, but they were too small for him to eat. We didn't know how to catch big ones, so he promised to show us how after dinner if Mom would let us.

Linda and I begged Mom to let us go after we ate fried chicken. We had to rig up a bunch of lines and hooks, walk the whole length of the creek, bait the hooks, and tie them along the water's edge. Gray didn't know anything about the creek, and no one else knew it better than us, so Mom allowed us to go.

We took off to the creek with a metal pail full of chicken livers, gizzards, and other raw chicken pieces. I carried the hooks and line we had wrapped around a pop bottle carton so they would not tangle. Gray carried a few beers and a flashlight in case it got dark. The creek was easier to walk since it had not rained in weeks, and you could jump the rocks to cross and not get your feet wet.

Gray told us to look for strong tree roots close to the water to tie the string and a sandy bottom creek bed. We knew the perfect spots. After I baited the huge hook with chicken liver, Linda swam in with the first line. Adjusting the string length just short of touching the bottom, she tied it off in the waterhole close to our spring water pipe before our shallow crossing point, which was almost dry.

We crossed the creek and headed up to the channel where the bass ran. There wasn't a good place to tie a line here, so we headed toward Walter's Pond. Gray helped us cross the rougher rapids where the saw grass was. This spot was perfect as the flood had washed a lot of soil under the trees, exposing their roots. The water level gave us a place to tie the lines.

As I baited the hooks, Linda swam across to tie lines along the bank. We tied the rest of our lines there rather than going on up to the turtle pond. We had been there a few weeks earlier, and it was almost dried up. Linda had me walk into the muddy pond for an old metal mop bucket to put crawdads in. When I came out, my legs were covered in leeches. Screaming as she pulled each one off, she assured me that I wasn't going to die. In fact, she used them to fish, placing each one into the bucket. She did this to all the other children each chance she got throughout the years, frightening them was pure enjoyment in addition to excellent fishing bait.

It was starting to get dark, so we headed back. Gray told us to keep an eye on the turtles and bait. If we caught one, he told us to put a stick in its mouth until we got it home. We had to keep the turtles in a washtub until he was able to come and pick them up.

As we got close to home, we could hear Dad playing music on the guitar, and everyone was singing. As Dad entertained us with music, we took turns jumping rope while the others caught lightning bugs until bedtime.

Chapter 13

The morning came early, and we hurried to do our chores. After having breakfast and grabbing turtle bait, Linda and I headed out to check our hooks. The first hook was not even touched. Gray said it would take time for the turtle to bite, and it wasn't as simple as fishing. So we headed up to check the others. The other lines were tight except one, so Linda swam in and baited it. The others were not touched as well. It was clear that something had eaten one bait, which assured us that we would catch something soon; we just had to keep trying. We headed back home to help Mom with some canning.

When we got home, Mom sent us to the garden to pick up all the cabbages. We washed them first and then shredded them in a large pot. While Mom prepared the mason jars and lids for sauerkraut, Linda and I went out and built a fire in the pit for the washtub.

Mom and Vickie came out shortly with the filled jars to be canned. They placed them in the tub and filled it with water. Plus, they wrapped each jar in old rags so they would not touch. We lifted it onto the bricks above the fire and watched it heat and begin to boil. When it was done and the lids indicated they were sealed, we put the fire out and let the water and jars cool down.

I never liked sauerkraut or coleslaw; I would rather eat raw cabbage. I knew I would not see any cabbage again after today until mid-summer of next year, and I dreaded the upcoming sauerkraut dinners.

For the next week, we would spend every day picking and canning everything left in the garden. We used to hold the smaller kids up to collect the peaches and ate the berries off the vines as soon as they ripened. There was no fruit for Mom to make jelly or jam. The cucumbers and tomatoes weren't so bad, since Mom worked on them in small batches as they came on, but all of us would have to help pick, string, and break the green beans.

The next day, Linda and I asked Danny to go with us to check the hooks. We had to get back to start on the beans and knew that would take the rest of the day, so saving time was important as well.

When we got up to the lines, we noticed a string was moving back and forth, and the tree root was stretched close to the water. We had finally caught a turtle. Gray did not tell us how to get the turtle out of the water or how hard it would be. We wrestled the line to untie it from the root and dragged it to the edge of the saw grass bank. The turtle was too big to lift, so we walked it downstream to the crossing and dragged it onto the bank. This turtle was huge and a snapper. I ran along the creek bank until I found a large stick to put in his mouth.

Gray had told us, "If the turtle bit you, it would not let go until a thunderstorm." Not knowing how much truth there was to that, we aggravated the turtle until it snapped and bit the stick. It wasn't letting go, and with its mouth gripped tight to the center of the stick, we were able to rest one end of the stick on Danny's shoulder and the other end on Linda's. Taking turns carrying and excited, we headed toward home.

We were exhausted when we finally arrived home; the front door was shut as we came. Mom was probably putting Billy Joe down for a nap, or she was mopping the floor. Linda decided to tie the turtle line to the door knob. Danny and I gathered the other kids and moved them to the side of the house. Reminding them all to be quiet, Linda ran up to the door, knocked, and ran over to where we all were. Ten little faces peeked around the side of the house, watching to see what would happen when she opened the door.

Hearing the knock on the door, she looked out the window first to see who was there. She thought maybe Donna or David was knocking since they were too short to open the door. As she opened the door, a big turtle leaped up at her, being pulled by the string with the stick still in its mouth. She slammed the door so hard that she let out a horrific scream. We then heard the glass break out of the front window. We were in trouble again.

After hearing us all laughing outside, she slowly opened the door with a broom in her hand and laughed at the sight of the turtle hanging there.

Throwing the broom at Linda, she said, “Clean that up! And the rest of you get ta pickin’ those beans!”

Chapter 14

My parents' friends, Vernon and Tootie, stopped in, as always, for the weekend. Meanwhile, Gray came to pick up the turtle. They laughed at what a good prank we had pulled on Mom. They laughed even harder at the window glass breaking. Mom, however, didn't think it was all that funny. After dinner and a few games of horseshoes, we all packed up our poles, bait, beers, and some blankets and headed down to the creek for some night fishing.

Danny, Linda, and I collected a large stack of wood off the creek bank and started a fire for light. The grownups, on the other hand, set their poles with chicken liver to bait a catfish.

Linda and I threw our poles and told Danny to watch our lines while we searched for more wood. Some of the kids sat on the blankets in front of Mom and Tootie, who were busy with Billy Joe. Gathering wood, I could see others playing in the shallow crossing, running back and forth, drinking from the spring by the light of the fire. Dad and Gray were catching fish pretty well on the liver and were collecting them onto a stringer. Linda and I decided to change the bait and went back for more wood.

Danny and Vernon started getting bites on their lines, too. Bam, Kay, and Donna were sitting on the water's edge, playing with the stringer of fish. Bam grabbed up the stringer for Vernon just as Linda and I added more wood to the fire. Lighting up the bank more, Linda screamed at Dad to get Donna.

She was face down, floating in the water along the edge of the bank. Who knew how long she was lying like this? The light from the fire reflecting the back of her leg caught Linda's attention. Dad grabbed her from the water in an instant and threw her lifeless body onto the bank.

Pushing on her chest and breathing into her mouth for minutes, she finally coughed and then spit up water—a lot of water. No one said anything this whole time. We were all frozen; we just watched. The night was still, and no one knew how, when, or why she got in the water.

I think when the commotion started with the fish, she tried to stand up. She perhaps stumbled backward and fell in. Linda and I blamed ourselves but also thought the grownups could watch for everyone since we were busy getting wood. Mom and Tootie decided to take the smaller ones and put them to bed and make sure Donna didn't need to go to the hospital.

Dad explained to us how to save someone like that. He mentioned not to take your eye off them while they swam. Linda and I didn't know how to save anyone, yet we figured with all the adults there, they should have been watching the kids. That's probably why Mom made the smaller ones stay home most of the time. Even when we had them, we were always teamed up.

We fished well into the night. Gray then cleaned all the fish and the turtle. We had decided to go fishing again and possibly frog gigging as he was coming back the next day. We taught Donna how to swim the following summer the same way we had taught others. However, it seemed she never liked and enjoyed water the way we all did.

Chapter 15

The creek was now almost dried up in many spots due to lack of rain. Meanwhile, school was about to start already. We had just received cards from the school regarding our new classroom and our teacher.

The days of fun were coming to an end, and we were not thrilled about it at all, certainly not as thrilled as Mom. She already had our school supplies organized and our clothes laid out. We would have to go try on those dreaded new school shoes in a few days at Gallenkamp, the local shoe store, and start going to bed a little earlier. I am sure that Mom welcomed the end of our daily circus. Nonetheless, we had a terrific summer, and somehow, we managed to save ourselves from severe injuries. Well, let's just say that we all survived.

I also received my "Finger Ding" doll in the mail, whose life was short-lived with all the other kids playing with it. I ordered two more dolls and hoped they would last longer.

The garden was done for the year. Potatoes were dug, turnips were out, and all that was left were a few pumpkins. Dad had already turned the soil and started clearing the patch of blackberry and raspberry vines from the front yard. With a large elongated piece of steel weighed down with tires and all us kids, he hooked it to the small tractor that he traded car work for. We rode for hours as he leveled the yard for grass seed. The yard looked nice, all opened up to the curve.

He cleared a large section on the other side of the lane up to the creek road for another garden next year, so Linda and I could sell more corn. Our cows and a pig or two would go to the butcher soon. Dad also talked about getting Linda a horse, as she was horse crazy! She rode everything that could carry her and always wanted a horse. She pleaded and promised to take care of it.

About a week after school started, the man from the creek that Mom shot at earlier that summer stopped by in his car while we were waiting for the bus. He rolled down the window and asked, "Do you want me to take you all to school? You won't have to stand there and wait."

We had already told Danny about the man and what he did to us at the creek. Danny recognized him for doing work on his car before and did not care for the man.

Danny reached down, picked up a rock from the lane, and threw it at his car. He said, "Get outta here, we don't need a ride."

Linda and I picked up rocks and threw them, and so did Vickie and Roberta, all the while yelling at him to leave.

After breaking a window, the man sped off as the school bus came to a screeching stop. After school, we told Mom and Dad what happened. Mom, being afraid he would steal one of us, told Dad and Danny to fix a car so we could drive to the bus stop. If he came back, we could get away, and we would not be standing there in the rain or the dark waiting for the bus.

We always had a car after that day. They were not the best of cars or, at times, complete cars; nonetheless, everyone on the school bus envied us. Danny drove the car in the mornings since we were usually late. However, he allowed Linda or me to drive it back home after school for driving practice. I enjoyed the absence of the daily trudge up and down the long lane through the mud holes and the winter snow.

I remember the walnuts falling from the trees and covering the side and back yard. We all spent days picking them and throwing them into the driveway to get the outer casing smashed. Once that was done, we all sat on the porch and cracked them open with hammers or rocks. All this effort was to put it in a jar for cookies or cakes alongside having a good time talking, laughing, and smashing our fingers. We would go to school with stained fingers for days and hated stepping on any broken shells that lay astray.

When the field corn was ready to be harvested, we climbed the fence next to the house and picked as much as we could. We then grated it down on a homemade grit board that Dad had made by punching holes into a piece of metal and mounting it to a wood frame with the rough side out. We raked the hard corn across it, as well as our knuckles, until we had enough meal for cornbread. It was the best cornbread ever made!

One day, Dad was at the work table making an extra board. Linda was playing around, of course, putting a whole kernel of corn in her nostril, pinching the other side. She was shooting the kernel at the others on the porch. Reva tried this but put kernels in both nostrils. Breathing in, they were sucked way inside her nose. Watching her struggle to breathe, we yelled for Mom, who screamed for Dad, not knowing what to do. He tried getting them out of her nose by using a paper clip. This required a hospital visit. They did not know what Linda was doing earlier and thought Reva was just being a kid, not copying what her big sister was doing.

Many of our birthdays were in October. Mom soon realized a round cake, cut into eight pieces, was not big enough to feed thirteen people. Besides, we were getting older now, and we all loved cake.

We made our own Halloween costumes and collected as much candy as we could since the smaller kids stayed home. Dad would drive us to a neighborhood with many houses, and we canvassed the area as fast as we could run, ringing doorbells and collecting candy. We would be finished in an hour, and he would then drive us to the next location. We all shared with the smaller kids, but finding a place to hide the rest of our candy in our small house was a challenge.

The days were shorter now, and winter was just around the corner. We were wearing our shoes and playing very little at the creek. We knew that once it was cold enough to freeze over, we would be down there skating. Packing coal in by the buckets, we kept quite warm at night. It was a routine duty to make a fire in the morning before leaving for school. During the big snows, Stanley Walter would bring his big tractor to plow the snow and dig us out. He created huge banks of snow on the sides of the lane so that we could hide during our snowball fights.

Dad would do minimal work on cars in the winter and spend most evenings watching TV with us. He would tell us stories about his music days and the times he played with the people on the "Hee Haw" television show. I remember "The Waltons", "Laugh-In", and "The Wonderful World of Disney" were on during our bath times, and the holiday cartoons were never missed. The "Aldens" Christmas catalog was the most looked-at book at this time. We would rip the toy pages out and save them as our wish list.

I spent most evenings teaching the smaller kids how to read from catalogs and books. I believe they all could pretty much read before they ever started first grade. Linda would study horse books that she had checked out of the library at the big school that she and Danny were going to now. She never finished her homework, and I would have to do it for her. I pretty much had to do all of her homework assignments until the day she graduated.

Chapter 16

Spring was finally on its way. Dad had decided to get Linda a horse rather than more cows. One day, we came home from school, and there she was, a beautiful brown quarter horse with a black mane and tail. She had a small white star on her face and black socks. Linda worked with her daily. She named her "Beauty" because of her elegance, and in no time, she was a gentle giant to us.

Linda never kept her in the fence pen outback. The need to mow grass was over now. Mom, however, grew tired of the manure piles in the grass and suggested we make a deal with the farmer across the road. So, Linda and I walked up to Stanley Walter's farmhouse and asked him if she could keep Beauty in his pasture. He had acres of pasture land for his cattle and a large barn. Thus, keeping Beauty was not going to be an issue for him.

He said with a chuckle, "No problem, girls. I'm glad you all decided to get a horse instead of trying to ride those cows."

Then, he said, "You might have trouble catching her. The fields go on for miles. Hmm, tell you what, you figure that out and you can keep her over there. Once a week, I ask, can you ride the fence line and help look for a broken fence?"

Linda said, "I can teach her to come to me, and I'll check your fences every day. She's fast."

Stanley laughed and said, "Okay then, but just check it once a week. That should be fine, and make sure the gate stays locked."

Running home, Linda never stopped talking about her new riding spot, and I thought, *Sure... that horse is going to come to you. Good luck!*

It took her two days. Every morning, Linda put a handful of oats in a small pail and put it in the car before we rode up the lane to get on the bus. After school, she'd crossed the street with the pail, shake it, and make a "click-click" noise at the gate and wait. Within minutes, Beauty would run to her. Feeding her the oats from her hand, Linda would walk her out of the gate, shut it, and cross the street. Throwing her school shoes and socks into the pail and grabbing her mane, Linda would jump onto her back and make that "click-click" noise. Beauty would go down the lane to get her saddle and bridle in the outbuilding.

Linda would ride Beauty every day after school for an hour. She also gave rides to others, three at a time, while I did her homework. On Saturday, Linda would ride the fence line, rain or shine, and report anything she found to Stanley. The farmer was surprised at how she had taught her horse and respected her determination to keep her promise. He never expected such focus from young Linda.

We would get the two gardens planted, and school would be over for the year. Linda would spend a lot of time with Beauty, and I, many times, would ride on the back. We still found time for the creek with others fishing. It was fun how Beauty followed us around like a large dog.

My grandparents came in for a couple of weeks at the beginning of summer to help finish the addition. Dad had a whole crew of men stop and help frame and put up the roof during the weekend. While Linda checked the fence line, I helped Grandpa with measuring the interior walls. It was he who taught me how to use the tape measure and the power tools.

When Linda was done, she stopped to get Grandma and me to go fishing. She rode Beauty through the woods to the field atop the fishing hole and tied her up to graze. Meanwhile, I walked through the woods on a streambed with Grandma. Linda cut down a path we made down to the creek, and we fished for a while. The neighbor boys showed up to swim, but since we were fishing, they sat down to watch. Grandma drank the two beers she had snuck out of the house from Grandpa. The two boys offered her more at their house.

Linda and I knew Grandpa and Mom didn't want her to drink. We saw the drinking bar at the boys' house last summer. We knew it would be trouble, but Grandma reeled her pole and followed the boys down the creek.

Linda took our fishing poles and told me to follow Grandma while she climbed up the creek bank to get Beauty. We got to the boys' house and helped Grandma up the new footpath next to the landfill Dad had made.

Linda rode up, tying the bridle off on a small tree. She said, "We have to leave; we can't stay here long."

Grandma agreed, and we all went inside. Their mother was watching TV and did not hear us come in. Their father, Ernie, stood up from his recliner chair and laid his newspaper down.

He said, "Hello, who is this?" as he extended his hand out for a handshake. Grandma said, "Hi, I'm Phyllis' mother. I've been down at the creek fishing with the girls and got a little thirsty."

He said, "What do you need? We have water, pop, or beer. Do you want a beer? Come on back and sit down, it's hot out there. Have a drink."

Linda and I talked to the boys for a while, and one of their brothers pulled up in a car. His name was Gary, and he was older than us. We had seen him last summer when Dad was working on their landfill, but we never spoke to him. Linda and he talked a lot, and I swore they were both smitten with one another. Linda denied it.

We went in the house to get Grandma since it was getting close to dinner time, and we had to get back.

"Oh no!" I said. "What are we going to do? She is so drunk that she can't even walk! Grandpa is not going to like this."

Grandma started to laugh and said, with a slur, "Oh yeah, I kin. I a ride ya horseback."

Linda said, "You can't even get up on it, let alone ride it."

I said, "Get her some coffee and let's try it. Mom will kill us."

We put a couple of cups of black coffee in her and tried to get her on the horse. Ernie suggested driving her home, but we decided to try to sneak her in.

It took many attempts for all of us to get her up on Beauty. Linda sat behind her to hold her on the saddle, and I, holding the reins, walked her through the cornfield toward home. Grandma held on, swaying. Each step the horse took was comical. Linda was telling her that we were in trouble. She told her she had to straighten up, but it made no difference at all since she was drunk!

We got to the yard, and I stopped Beauty at the "three trees" for Linda to get off. This was our BIG plan. I'd carry the poles and Linda would walk the horse to the back to the outbuilding while Grandma rode. We'd hang out there to take off the saddle and brush her down. You could hear Grandpa hammering there.

We took about ten steps past the "three trees", and Grandma fell off! I yelled and went to pick Grandma up. She spit into her hand and let out a laugh.

Opening her hand, she says, "I knocked out my tooth."

I looked at Linda and said with despair, "Now what?"

The other kids saw Grandma fall off and came running. We got Grandma to the picnic table and sat her down, telling them all to hush. We got to know that Mom was cooking. It was obvious that she would never leave the stove while she was cooking, so we sent them inside to snatch a wet towel and a blanket.

Bam went in and said, "Grandma knocked her tooth out. She fell off the horse. I need a wet towel."

Mom asked, "Is she all right? What's she doing on that thing anyway? That Linda! I'm going to have her head! She must have done something." She tended the stove.

Bam came out with a wet towel, and we cleaned Grandma's face up and laid her on the blanket to sleep it off. She slept a good hour and appeared fine when she woke, except for her missing tooth. She told Mom she thought she could stay on... sure, she did. She could do anything as drunk as she was; we wouldn't have been surprised.

Grandma would frequent the neighbor's home, and we would eventually be unable to hide her. Dad or Danny drove down to save her from getting hurt. Grandpa stopped complaining around us. He wasn't happy; he just stopped complaining.

Grandpa had finished the house addition shell before heading back to Hazard. Once completely done, it would provide us with much more needed space. There were two bedrooms with closets and a large closet at the end of the hall. He closed the side door to the house and opened a large space in the wall of the living room to the new hallway. We had a second front door and a large living room. Mom always wanted a large living room and a picture window. Now, she would have it once the room was finished.

Midsummer, Dad had traded car work for an awning-style porch, and Vernon and Gray helped put it on the house over the concrete slab. It was too short for the house and the slab. However, it provided plenty of shade and a place to sit during the rain. That is why it was useful in its own way.

Danny had gone to Hazard again for the summer, and Dad traded a car and some cash for a school bus and converted it into a camper for our travel down this year. There was plenty of space for all of us, yet the cost to drive such a large vehicle so far was too expensive. So, he traded it for a late 50s diesel Greyhound bus converted to a camper.

The bus needed a lot of interior work as well as motor work. However, it was ready to go by the following summer. Linda and I treated it as our home, and Danny drove it back to the outbuildings. We worked on it daily with paint, and Mom made the mini curtains. We all painted the outside a red, white, and blue scheme using brushes, and with the name "Browning's" in the destination window, it was ready to travel.

Dad sent our last two pigs to the butcher in the fall and found us a small black Welsh pony. We named it "Weeny" and kept it with her horse. Dad simply gave us something else to ride. We tried many other ponies and sold them before he got this one, and we were able to train it like the horse.

Having Beauty and Weeny, Linda and I had traveled everywhere in the three-mile radius of our house at this time and frequented our small town. Everyone in town knew us due to the horse and the many trails we had made through the creek and woods to get to town. We would fish every spot along the creek and swim the horse and pony, if need be, to get to the other side.

Dad told us we could go anywhere as long as we stayed off the road, and that we did.

Chapter 17

By then, Linda and I were in junior high school. On Tuesdays, we would ride the school bus home to our girlfriend Rhonda's house during the winter. Her parents belonged to a bowling league, and we would help her babysit her little brother. She lived in a small subdivision. We enjoyed walking around and visiting many of the people we knew from school.

Her parents would order us pizza and pay her ten dollars for watching her brother, who was already six years old. That made no sense to me at all; why couldn't we just cook our own food? Plus, why did she get paid to watch her little brother? Isn't that a family thing? We would get to her house and take off our shoes since they had carpeted floors. However, we never put them back on as we walked the neighborhood. Her mother would complain about how black our feet were from blacktop streets and constantly told us to wear our shoes, but we didn't listen.

Another friend of ours, Tina, lived two streets over. We would frequent her house when we stayed with Rhonda. Tina and Rhonda were both into fashion. They stayed up-to-date with hairstyles and makeup, while Linda and I couldn't care less. I was glad to have broken my black-framed glasses at a distant neighbor girl's barn and wore a gold wire frame pair now. Yet, one night, Rhonda pierced our ears using an ice cube and a safety pin. I still have trouble with earrings in my left ear. Linda never had trouble and always wore horseheads or cowboy boots in hers.

Rhonda's mother had a portable sewing machine, and after using the one at school, I was pretty good at sewing. It was so much easier to use than Mom's treadle machine. I was able to make our flare-bottom jeans with a flannel material insert. If our jeans weren't dragging the ground, I would add a two-inch strip to the length. We were in style!

Since Linda and I paid for our clothes using the money we made selling corn, we didn't make many pairs of flared jeans and just borrowed Rhonda's. The hard shoes finally became history and were replaced with the comfort of the popular black Converse tennis shoes. They weren't practical on rainy days, but our style outweighed our soaking-wet feet. The colorful, wide-legged flares mimicked a sponge as we sloshed around their neighborhood, knowing we were looking good.

They would talk on the phone to boys in the neighborhood for hours. On the other hand, I never really paid much attention to any of them when I got to school. They all seemed too childlike. Looking back now, they were actually normal for their age; we were just used to doing things our way by now.

Rhonda and Tina rode the school bus home with us to stay for the weekend. We were going to fish, ride horses, and spend the night in the bus camper for the weekend since it was the start of our spring break. Linda and I could double up on the horse, but two people couldn't ride the pony. Weeny would carry them, but it would not be good for her since she was a small pony. Rhonda and Tina, being from what they called "the city", were naïve. Linda came up with the idea of getting more ponies for the weekend.

We had seen three ponies across the creek in a fenced-in, overgrown field last summer. We frequented the property, and intense exploration concluded that it must have been an old homestead and its demise was due to Indiana attacks.

The property had a house and a barn at one time many years ago, and only the creek rock basement remained. Old rough-cut boards covered the hand-dug well holes we stumbled upon while combing the property. Taking hours to clear a patch of raspberry vines, we uncovered a small creek rock formation built into the side of a grassy hill, possibly an old spring house used for cold storage. The wood from its roof had rotted away, leaving old nails. Hardware from what appeared to have come from an old door lay on the rock floor of the structure, as well as a few arrowheads.

We had fed the ponies apples, and Linda had ridden them bareback. They were very well-natured, and with a little care, Linda was sure Rhonda and Tina would be able to ride them. We just had to get them. After dinner and our chores, we all took off across the creek and walked around the large cornfield edge, where the soil was freshly turned. We found a loose section of the fence and removed the rusty U-shaped nails from the old wooden post. We carefully folded down the fence low enough for the ponies to get out without looking too deliberate. With hay string for a lead rope, we walked the ponies back along the large cornfield edge to the creek. We walked them down the tractor road near the big fishing hole crossing the creek to our creek road.

Out of sight from Mom, Dad, and the others, we led them to our outbuilding up the path we had made at the end of the garden. We brushed and cleaned them up by cutting their mane and tail. Linda trimmed their hooves since they were overgrown. We worked with them all night, and by morning, Linda had them ready to ride.

Mom never went back to the fenced pens, and it was our job to tend the animals. We went up to the house for breakfast and told Mom that we were going to ride and fish all day. Vickie and Berta were helping a lot more, and with Reva, Bam, and Kay already going to school, Donna, David, and Billy Joe were easier to watch.

The other two ponies just followed Beauty and Weeny down the path at the end of the garden toward the creek. We had locked the other one in the outbuilding in case one of the others couldn't keep up. Still out of sight of Mom, we took off downstream through the creek and up the tractor road toward town. We rode all day and well into the evening before going home for dinner and locking them away.

After dinner and dishes, Rhonda and Tina did their typical primping to impress the boys. We spent all night fishing with Timmy and Jimmy at the fishing hole. We had finally dragged ourselves home and went to bed just short of daybreak. Around noon, Mom was knocking on the door of the bus for Linda to get up.

Linda rubbed her eyes, and Mom asked, “What did you all do? Stay up all night?”

In a groggy voice, Linda answered, “Yeah, what do you need?”

Mom said, “There are some people here. They are looking for three ponies. Have you seen them? They mentioned they are from across the creek.”

I almost died, as did Rhonda and Tina. Putting my hand over my mouth, I signaled them to be quiet. I knew Linda would be able to handle it. I didn't know how, but I knew she'd come up with something.

Linda said, “Yeah, found them last night drinking water in the creek while we were fishing. We put them in the pen and fixed them. Their hooves were bad, and their mane too. We also fed them.”

The man and woman were grateful and thanked us. In fact, they handed Linda fifty dollars for caring for them. We were excited as we weren't going to jail for stealing. We got up and rode the ponies back across the creek to their fence and helped the couple repair it where we broke it down.

Chapter 18

School was out for the week, and Linda had already ridden Beauty for the day. Linda and I tried fishing, but we weren't able to catch anything. We decided to walk up to visit with Timmy and Jimmy. Arriving at their house, we noticed that they were next door to their neighbors, the Locks. They lived in the same driveway in a two-story, stucco-type home. It was somewhat elevated in case of flood water from the creek. They had a large side yard and played baseball often.

We had played there a few times in the past. Normally, I would play dolls with the girl, Pammy, inside while they played baseball with the boys. I didn't like the game at all because I always got hit in the head with the ball by the other boys, and I didn't want to break my glasses. Besides, it just hurt.

Instead of playing baseball that day, they all just hung out in the front yard. Pammy's younger brother, Kevin, was riding a playground-style seesaw in their front yard with Linda. While Linda was in the air, he decided to jump off and laugh. Linda came plummeting down, and when she hit the ground, her foot twisted underneath the board. Her face also hit the metal T-bar handle.

Splitting her bottom lip open, Linda came off the seesaw, ready to beat him up, but realized her ankle was hurt. She was unable to walk now. They came inside to get me and some ice for the swelling. We decided to head home. Gary had just come home as I was helping her limp past their house. He asked what happened to Linda's foot, and I told him. We then made our way through their backyard into the large field toward home.

About midway through the freshly turned field, Linda and I heard yelling and looked up at the road; we saw Gary and Jimmy in his small European car pulling into the lane. Gary was driving too fast when he pulled into the lane, but when he tried hitting the brakes, the brake line broke. Unable to slow the car down, he turned the wheel too sharp at the curve where we would park our car every morning before school. The car skidded in the gravel and then flipped onto its side. Jimmy was holding on to the window edge when it flipped, and the car slid across the gravel, trapping his hand for quite a distance before coming to a stop.

Danny had heard the noise while he was working on a lawn mower and drove up the lane to help get the car upright and get Jimmy out. Linda and I had made it through the field and out of our path through the woods just as Danny and Jimmy came driving down the lane. He needed a hospital. You could see the bones in the top of his hand with pieces of gravel embedded inside. His shirt was already saturated in blood, and he had wrapped it to try to stop the bleeding.

Leaving the car running in front of the house, Danny ran inside to get Mom to take Jimmy to the hospital and get a fresh towel for the blood. I walked up, supporting Linda when Mom came out of the house. As soon as Mom saw the blood, she passed out. In a crisis as to what to do next and Gary too shaken to drive, we wrestled Mom into the back seat of the car. As she lay limp, Danny drove off with Jimmy.

Danny was driving at only thirteen and a half years old while Jimmy gave him directions to the hospital. Mom had awakened by the time they arrived at the hospital and almost passed out again, knowing Danny had driven there without a license. Mom had recently gotten her license, yet never went anywhere except for the store. She got it in case of an emergency and passed out when she faced one. Gary's car was destroyed, and Jimmy's hand would require numerous surgeries before he was able to use it again. Gary was delivering the lighter Linda had left at the Locks' house when she got hurt. I knew it then; it was clear that he was smitten with her.

Chapter 19

It was usual to pass the roller-skating rink on our trips to town. We had no interest in it at all until Rhonda and Tina found it to be the perfect opportunity to meet the boys from their neighborhood. Rhonda and Tina would ride the school bus home with us every Friday until school let out for the year. After our dinner and chores, we would walk to the rink through the fields and the paths we had made through the woods. They would flirt around with the young boys while Linda and I concentrated on the art of roller skating.

We met an older man who lived upstairs and maintained the floors there. He was an excellent skater and taught us everything from how to race to the waltz. We would frequent the rink every night it was open and spent many Sundays there. On Sunday, Linda and I would ride Beauty up and leave her in the small field next to the rink if we weren't working in the garden. The crowd was smaller, and the man could teach us more.

Rhonda and Tina didn't visit much during the summer, and we would just meet up at the rink. Sometimes, Rhonda was able to spend the weekend and would meet her older sister at her boyfriend's house, who lived near the rink. Grandma and Grandpa came in for their usual couple-week visit and managed to finish the rooms in the house. It was nice to have our own bedroom, but Linda and I knew it would seem small again when Rhonda and Tina came for a sleepover. The outside addition still required siding, and Mom's living room lacked furniture. However, a large queen-sized bed sat in it for an extra sleeping room. Danny got the other bedroom and shared it with David, who was four, and Billy Joe, who was three years old.

The bedroom was nice, as I said. However, the window was too small for us to get in and out of for our all-night fishing ventures with the neighbor boys. We grew accustomed to such plans with the camper bus. We had to use the window now since Dad recently sold the bus. Dad would constantly remind us not to slam the door.

With two front doors and the back door blocked off with a double bed, Linda's creativity kicked in. She cut a doorway into the outer wall of the house in Danny's bedroom. We blocked the opening with a large antique dresser on casters. We were able to come in for bed in the evening and slip back out for more fishing at night without making any noise. That was it; we got what we wanted, thanks to Linda’s idea.

In need of an outdoor sleeping spot for the summer, Linda and I cleared a spot of land next to the creek atop the bank near our shallow crossing spot just past the outbuildings. Slowly removing building materials from Dad's collection daily, we managed to build a two-story clubhouse with an observation deck. Our house had two rooms for sleeping and a living room area that we furnished with two bench seats from an old car Dad was parting out.

With secret latches on the door, we were able to hang out with the boys at the creek, and Mom could not get in. Us being of the “know-it-all teenager stage”, never thought once about her knowing exactly what was going on and what we were up to, as I am sure she did. We thought that she would assume we were sleeping when we didn't answer the door.

Danny had his friends coming over often to tinker with cars and lawnmowers. They would stay the night to go fishing. Between the neighbor boys and his friends, our creek house became the happening spot for the summer.

All of us were still up to our own shenanigans, keeping Mom on her toes. Reva managed to bounce off the big queen bed in the new living room and split her head wide open, requiring thirteen stitches. Dad had fixed a big tractor, and while he was disking the ground for one of the large gardens, Reva fell off, and he drove over her. Luckily, she was so small. She fit between the disks and had only scraped her shoulders and hips.

Danny, Linda, and I helped Dad paint the tractor a bright orange color so he could sell it. We finished painting and took some gasoline and soap to the creek to wash the oil-based paint off our skin. While we were down there, Bam and David decided to paint their entire bodies orange before Mom caught them. This would take gallons of gasoline to remove. Their skin was about to fall off their bones by the time we were finished cleaning them up.

Danny had gotten another surgery on his eye. Shortly after arriving home from the hospital, Linda got him onto Beauty for a ride carelessly, in which he fell off again. Mom was livid, but somehow, he came out fine.

Dad had created a flood barrier wall of trees a few summers back along the edge of the property near the creek road using the dozer. He was talking about building a garage on the old two-story foundation next spring. He wanted to be sure that floodwater would not get up to it. We all would run the tree trunks back and forth for entertainment. It continued like this until Bam lost her footing one day and fell into a hidden honeybee nest, resulting in hundreds of bee stings. Vickie pulled her out and rolled her into our muddy pond that Dad had tried to make, which saved her life.

I stepped on the end of a broken pop bottle at the creek and knew it was bad when I felt the heat of the glass inside my foot. Yelling for Linda to pull it out, she wrapped her shirt around it and helped me limp home. I had punctured the entire arch of my left foot. With my fear of stitches, I assured Mom that I didn't need them and Linda would take care of me. Spending about half the summer on my tip toes and white bandages around my foot, I was limited to the creek bank or on the pony until it healed.

Our cousin, Amy, and her friend, Beth, ran away from home and showed up at the creek one evening while we were fishing. We did not know why they ran away then, but we enjoyed hanging out with her and meeting her friend. They spent the night in our creek house. When Mom came back, asking Linda if she had seen them that morning, she said, “No.”

We snuck them over to the far corner of one of the fields across the creek and made them a shelter out of an overgrown thicket of brush. A few days later, we were tired of all their demands for food, blankets, candles, and such. We carelessly allowed Mom to catch us taking them food. I felt bad for Aunt Duck and her desperation to find her. We were taught not to rat on people, but we were mad at Amy for getting us involved.

Chapter 20

Danny and Linda were in high school now, and I was in the eighth grade. Our bus schedules were different than the others. So, we still drove a car up and down the lane. Mom would drive the other six children. David and Billy Joe were home all day, though. With so many children in school, I became the household school activity secretary at this time.

Every note was written by me and so was every permission slip on file. From the absences, field trips, and bus passes to the detentions Danny and Linda received, everything was written with a quick, creative hand. I had mastered Mom's signature, and the interception of the mail was frequent. The detentions were easily evaded by indicating the lack of a telephone and the inability to leave the small children at home.

Linda was starting to spend more time talking to Gary, and I could sense that Jimmy was interested in me. I knew Dad would not approve of us dating the neighbor boys due to such a large age difference. So, I carefully kept a distance. Timmy, on the other hand, was my age, and after he stood on my back, pinning me underwater, I never cared for him. Linda, however, didn't see the eight-year age difference as a problem; she and Gary began to date secretly.

Using Rhonda, me, and the roller rink as a cover, they drove around and picked us up at closing. As long as we came in together, we figured Mom had no idea what was going on.

One evening, we got ready for the rink and walked to Gary's house. Loading into his car, he and Linda drove up and dropped

Rhonda and me off to skate. It had rained a little while we were inside. However, with Gary giving us a ride home, I welcomed the lack of mud on the bottom of my jeans.

Rhonda and I closed the rink. I spent the whole time skating with the old man there. Without Linda, I was able to practice the waltz more. Rhonda just flirted around as usual. After walking out and waiting about 15 minutes for Gary and Linda to show, we decided to start walking home. They were late or had forgotten to pick us up, but we would stop at Gary's to get her before walking on in.

Sloshing through the trails, our big, flared jeans and tennis shoes were soaked from the earlier rain. Rhonda and I decided to cut through a yard to get onto our street a couple of houses from Gary's driveway. The street was deserted at night, and knowing I wasn't allowed to walk it, Rhonda and I walked faster. We saw headlights from a car coming behind us. We stopped walking for a brief moment, believing Gary and Linda were coming from the rink to pick us up.

This was not the case. In a split second, the car stopped. Two grown men got out and grabbed us. Throwing us into their small car, they took our roller skates and threw them into the ditch before taking off. They were laughing and hollering as if they had just caught their prey on a hunting trip while I was panicking.

I was in the back seat with the older man. I thought about the man at the creek, the bus stop, and the possibility of one of these three being him. They drove close to our lane. I could see Gary's car parked at the top. Linda and he were waiting for us. I told the driver to pull in there.

The driver, a much younger man than the others, hesitated. Then he sped up and said, "There is a car parked there!"

I said, "It's okay. It's my sister and her boyfriend."

The older man said to the driver, "That won't work. Keep going."

I looked forward at the driver and over at Gary's car as they drove past. Rhonda, from the front seat, turned and looked at me. I didn't know what to do, nor did she.

They drove for miles down my street, and I remained focused on the creek. If I got a chance to get out of this car, I could get home by following it without a problem, and Rhonda had better run with me.

They pulled off the road and drove down a long gravel lane before stopping. The other man in front, about twenty-five years old, got out, grabbed a beer, and walked off to relieve himself, telling the others to hold on to us. When the dome light inside the car came on, I could get a better look at them.

They had this "wannabe rockstar look", long, wiry hair, yet their faces were clean-shaven. They were wearing blue jeans and a simple T-shirt. The man in the back with me was sloppy fat. The man came back and told us to take off our shoes and socks. He grabbed them, threw them out of the car, and laughed. "They won't be able to run without these," he said as he drank from the beer bottle and got back into the car.

Rhonda talked to the men about just anything, and it seemed to help. With her makeup, she appeared much older than me. She was used to talking to older people. I thought those men might possibly know her older brother and sister by their closeness in age. I was busy reading road signs and landmarks to help us get away while she talked and drank some of their beer. I didn't drink, and the man in the back with me kept trying to get me to, spilling it on my clothes and down my face.

I tuned out a lot of what was being said and thought of the old man at the skating rink. He reminded us to be careful going home when we decided to take off walking.

"We are walking the trails," I said with assurance. "We'll be fine. See you tomorrow."

Thoughts raced through my head. *Why did I get on the road?* Then, I was mad at Linda for being late. *Why did these men steal us?* Now, I was scared thinking about what they were going to do to us.

They drove us through the country for hours that night before pulling into a quick-stop market for more beer. I told the younger man who was driving that I had to use the bathroom. The fat man from the back seat reached forward and held a knife to Rhonda's throat to ensure I didn't scream for help.

I walked into the market, toward the back to the restrooms, my wet, soggy jeans brushing across the cold tile floor beneath my bare feet, wanting the clerk to approach me for not having shoes on. He was too busy at the register to notice, and that opportunity for help was exhausted. I went back to the car. I couldn't leave Rhonda.

Reality had now set in; we were in deep trouble, and I couldn't help but still be angry at Linda for not picking us up. The man at the rink was the last one who saw us, and no one knew where we were. We did not know where we were, and these men were drunk, and their intentions were not pleasant.

We left the market, and I was focused even more on the road signs. The driver made two more turns before pulling into a dry creek bed, parked the car, and made us get out. I recognized this place and knew we were far from home. I explored this creek bed with Rhonda on one of our trips with her sister and her boyfriend. He raced his dirt bike in the motocross race at the top of the hill nearby, and we walked the area out of boredom.

Pretending to have to use the restroom again and asking for privacy, the fat man stepped away from me. The driver argued with the others to leave us alone and suggested just leaving us there, but with us knowing their names at this point, the fat man from the back seat was reluctant. I turned my back to him and acted as if I was undoing my pants. I crouched down and took off running. Yelling for Rhonda to run and not looking back, I took off down the creek bed and up a short bank, my feet slipping a few times before reaching the top as I ran toward a porch light in the distance. I yelled again for Rhonda in the middle of a large grassy field riddled with briars and was relieved to hear her voice from behind me.

"Keep running, they're coming!" she said.

We reached a small subdivision and ran to the house with the light on. Knocking repeatedly on the door, an elderly gray-haired man opened it. There we stood. From his expression, we must have been a sight, and I asked,

"May we use your telephone?"

Without question, he invited us in, and I tried calling Gary's house many times, but no one answered. I assured Rhonda I knew where we were, and we thanked the man and left his home. We had a lot of walking to do, and it was three in the morning.

Standing on the porch, the men drove by and saw us. He stopped the car at the corner and waited. I knocked on the door again. The old man opened the door, dressed, with his car keys in hand, and offered to take us home.

We declined the ride many times and, being covered in mud and wet, did not want to ruin his new car. His wife calmed us down and told us we would be fine. The men were still waiting at the corner when we pulled out, and I finally felt safe.

He said to us, "You girls look as if you've been through a lot tonight. I'm not going to ask any questions unless there's something I need to know or help you with."

I assured him we were fine, and some men tried to hurt us, so we ran away. I expressed our gratitude for him saving us, to which he replied, "You saved yourselves by running. Should I have called the police?"

I said, "No, they will probably come back and get us for sure then. We're okay. I just want to forget about it."

With that said, we were all silent. He drove us to Millville, about 15 miles away, and when I asked to stop near the bridge in town, we got out. Rhonda and I could get home from there through the creek. I didn't want to burden him any longer after all that he had done.

We walked about ten feet, and the old man pulled up next to us and said, "You girls don't live here. Get in. I am taking you home."

Exhausted and cold, we got in, and he drove us to the lane. He dropped us off at the top, and we promised him we lived there. After many thanks and a hug, he drove off. He saved our lives.

Realizing we were safe, I thought back and smiled. We outran them big old drunks, and their idea of taking our shoes and our inability to run without them was their big plan. What a joke!

We finally walked down the lane. The sun would be coming up within an hour, and Dad would be waking up. We walked behind the house, snuck through our homemade door in the back, and crawled into bed, dirty clothes and all.

Linda asked, "Where have you been?"

I just whispered, "We'll tell you later." I heard Dad getting up before falling asleep.

Linda covered for us that morning and did the chores. She told Mom we were sick from walking home in the wet trails and needed sleep. When we woke up, Rhonda and I had hidden our muddy clothes and changed the bedsheets before Mom could notice.

We had piled the sheets in with the other dirty laundry. Mom had been dropping us off at the laundromat at this time on Sunday afternoons, and we would just clean them then.

Linda, Rhonda, and I walked up to the road to get our roller skates, but the water had ruined the bearings. I made Linda pay for new ones, and with the help of the old man at the rink, my skates rolled like a fine-tuned military machine. I told Linda to tell Mom about her and Gary because I wasn't going to die. After all, she wanted to sneak around.

I don't believe she ever told Mom then, but she was never late again.

Chapter 21

Dad had started building his garage. He noticed that all of his materials were gone. When he questioned Linda and me about the whereabouts, we could only respond by suggesting he look at what we had built. He was impressed by our two-story creek house, and with a shrug of his shoulders, he said, "They were just going to lay there and rot anyway."

Grandma and Grandpa would be coming in to help build the garage, and the siding on the house would wait another year. We were excited about our homemade door not being closed in. Danny was happy to finally be getting a garage to work out of.

We still had the gardens, chickens, Beauty, and Weeny, but our interests were changing. Danny finally got his driver's license. Our ancient poles had long been replaced with the popular Zebco 202, but finding the time to fish was scarce.

Dad had taken on a night watchman job at the junkyard on Friday, Saturday, and all day on Sunday, in addition to the foundry. Mom would take him to dinner with one or two of the kids at about six and arrive home at about ten in the evenings. On Sundays, Mom would drop us off at the laundromat, and Danny would come to pick us up.

I was finally in high school and at that awkward freshman stage. I had thrown the ridiculous flared-bottom jeans away after the kidnapping—should that ever happen again, I would be able to run even faster. The brother of the older man from the front seat sat behind me in my homeroom class, and I cringed every morning at the sight of him and had to bite my tongue.

He was absent one day, and a different boy, last name Casey, sat in his seat. The boy had spoken to me in the past, but today, I paid him no mind, trying to get my school papers and Linda's together. I would meet her every morning and hand her the homework that I completed during the last period's study hall the day before.

In his attempt to get my attention, he threw a ball of chewing gum into my hair. I turned around in my seat to hit him, and he jumped, laughed, and moved back to his original seat. I met Linda, gave her the completed homework, and pointed to the boy as he walked by, laughing.

She looks at me and says, "It's not that bad. Don't worry about it."

I grew tired of trying to get it out throughout the day and cut the chunk out in my Home Economics class, which left a large gap in my long hair. I was mortified, and that evening, Linda tried fixing it to no avail. She had cut my hair up to my neck. I never had my hair that short, and I cried and refused to go to school the next day.

She told me that she would fix it, and I screamed, "HOW? You can't put my hair back on."

She said, "Just wait!"

The next morning, we stopped at the store for our normal soda pop, and she bought a pack of bubble gum.

When the bell rang for class change, I met Linda with her homework, and she grabbed hold of the Casey boy by the head as he walked past. Covering his entire head in chewed-up bubble gum, she opened a locker door and pushed him inside.

She kicked the door of the locker and said, "Never touch her again. You got that?!"

He whimpered, "Yes, yes, got it."

This would get the whole school's attention as well as the office's. I wrote the letters and intercepted the mail for it, but it was well worth it. The Casey boy, however, had to shave his head, and that was not a cool look for school. I eventually got used to the short hairstyle, and with Rhonda's help styling it, I seemed to fit in.

On the other hand, the school system grew tired of all of us and gave Linda and me a job cleaning the school two hours a day in an attempt to keep us under some sort of control. We enjoyed the money, and we worked well together. Cutting up and playing around was normal for us, but the job got done.

I would get my period and confide in Linda for all the rules. In an era where this was not discussed openly like today, Linda left me confused for years. Her stories of not being able to swim because it was bad for the fish were untrue, and after day seven, a hospital visit was required. Her stories were ridiculous. Why did she do that to me? I would have told the other girls the truth, but the school system began showing a movie and required a signed permission slip from home for reviewing. I wrote Mom's signature on the form to keep Linda from tormenting them.

School let out for the summer, and we would work a forty-hour week. With that garden and the laundry, Linda's time was short for Beauty, and the need for a car forced her to sell her. I know her heart broke when she loaded her up, but those people bought the best horse ever raised.

A few weeks later, Weeny missed her and pushed open the gate to our outbuilding. She walked up the lane to the pasture across the road and was struck by a car. Suffering, Dad had to put her down. We never got another horse or a pony. It just hurt too bad; it hurt all of us.

Chapter 22

Linda bought a car and started driving. Our dangerous days riding with Danny were over now. We were still working for the school and frequenting the junkyard for parts and gasoline. After the laundromat on Sunday, Linda and I would spend the day there with Dad and Mom, fill our tank, and grab parts for my car, the 1968 Chevelle.

Dad bought me the body and, with instruction, taught me what I needed and how to put it together. If I took it off a car, I knew how to put it on my car. I was starting to become an interchange expert on Chevrolet and GM parts. I had another year and a half before I got my license, and I knew it would take me at least that long to get my project car up and running.

Linda would buy the cheap cars Gary would come across at the junkyard he worked at. She would have him fix and sell them, making crazy money. She was busy with a car once and awaiting parts; Dad gave her one of his projects. We drove that big 1966 four-door Oldsmobile to school. At the end of the day, we came out to start it, but it didn't start. Lifting the hood, we noticed that someone had stolen the battery.

Dad took on Wednesday nights at the junkyard, helping us with any midweek automobile crisis we encountered. We just put the battery in the night before after bumming a ride from Mom to the junkyard to get it and fill our gas tank by siphoning and filling about four five-gallon cans.

Stranded, we borrowed jumper cables from the twin boys, friends of Danny who frequented the house, and started the car in the school parking lot. We dropped Rhonda off at her house and went on to the school to clean. We had to leave the car running for two hours in the parking lot while we worked and barely had enough gas left to get home.

We rode to school with Danny the next day and bummed a ride to work. Mom picked us up there. We went on to the junkyard for another battery and more gas.

Saturday morning, after filling the tank and putting the new battery in, Danny and Linda discussed how to make sure someone didn't steal it again. Linda didn't agree with Danny's "who cares, just get another one" attitude and hated thieves.

She picked up a big chop axe from the garage, and with two large blows, she chopped two large holes into the hood of the car. She then dressed a heavy log chain Dad used for dragging logs with the bulldozer through the holes and around the bumper to secure it with a large padlock.

The car and its new hood ornament were the talk of the school on Monday. No one ever stole anything from us again. I believe that's when the Browning name was followed up with the words, "They are crazy!"

We never found out who stole the battery, and that's probably a good thing. We would still fish whenever possible. Dad finally found our homemade door. He was mad but agreed it was creative. He understood then why it was so hard to heat the house the past winter.

Amy ran away again, but rather than hiding at our house, she hid out at Danny's friends, the twins who helped us. Their father worked the third shift and welcomed a home-cooked breakfast when he came in from work. Their mother died during childbirth, and seemingly, her company helped fill the void. Their father questioned who she was and with some made-up story. He was none the wiser, and Aunt Duck had to track her down again.

With Linda driving, Rhonda and Tina were almost living with us. Our trips to the roller rink were to pick up the other kids. We had taught them to skate in the house, and the tile floor displayed an obvious circular path. Dad had replaced the coal stove with an oil furnace, and the fuel line lay across the kitchen and bedroom doorway. Linda told the kids that the house would explode if they hit the line. So, they learned to jump it and avoided breaking it.

Grandma and Grandpa had finally remodeled the kitchen and cabinets. Countertops replaced the large chest freezer. Mom had finally gotten furniture for her large living room and declared the room off-limits. And I do mean "OFF-LIMITS!" (It's a good thing because Danny caught a motorcycle on fire in it over the past winter and nearly burnt the whole house down.)

Grandpa was spending the evenings with Aunt Duck or Uncle Buggy, leaving Grandma for us to handle. She was still hiding her beer and managed to lose a few more teeth after visiting the neighbor's bar and falling into the bathtub. Grandma still followed the Reds on the radio. She was so excited to attend three home games using tickets I would receive for being an honor roll student. Uncle Buggy would take her since he was used to the big city traffic. The games became the highlight of her trip every summer.

Chapter 23

Danny and Linda were graduating this year. At this time, Danny spent his days in auto-mechanics class trying to teach the teacher. Linda lost her interest at the end of the year and slept in the first period while I completed her homework. She often skipped second-period class to go down the street from the school and slept at a pull-off near the creek. I wrote her notes indicating emergencies at home. The missed classes were dismissed.

Two weeks before they graduated, Danny was accused of skipping school one day. He was called a liar by the principal when he was home working on a car. After disrupting the entire school and scaring the principal to death, he walked out and did not finish. A couple of days later, Linda found she was pregnant. Mom made her finish the year and graduate.

Dad was essentially informed of Gary and Linda's relationship, and they got married in Mom's big living room. The reception was held in the front yard at the end of June and was a big deal. They managed to purchase the trailer in a mobile home park and struggled to make ends meet, awaiting their daughter Lucy's birth in early January. Gary left the junkyard and took a job at a casting foundry to better provide for them.

Danny got married and worked at the same foundry as Dad. In the evenings, he did side work out of the garage. They had a baby boy, only to find out a year later of her infidelity, and they divorced. He moved to Hazard and lived there for about three years, helping Grandma and Grandpa with things, and got a job driving a coal truck.

I was dating a man named Opey. With Danny and Linda out of the house, I seemed to be in a hurry to get out on my own. I was still cleaning the school at the time. I told Dad that I was going to move in with Opey rather than get married. There was a six-year difference in our ages. I managed to convince Dad that I didn't know what I was really doing and if it didn't work, I'd be back. He reminded me not to forget where I came from and to visit often. I laughed and thought, *I was just seven minutes away.*

Our bare feet were replaced with shoes. Linda and I still frequented the creek at every chance. Her long expeditions were cut short and limited to the length of the creek road. Linda was still able to spot the small turtles in the sand and skip a rock a good distance before it skipped across the bank on the other side. While fishing at the end of the footpath, we talked a lot about the baby coming, our dreams, and how fast the others were growing up as they swam upstream.

The chicken coop and our gardens were replaced with grass. The natural gas company had torn down our two-story creek house since it was built atop their line. Mom and Dad had a phone installed to keep in touch with those who left home. It rang off the hook for the others still there.

At the start of my senior year, I finished my car and got thrown out of auto mechanics class for punching the teacher after he smeared grease across my face. My creative mouth threatened to sue the school, and they allowed me to take wood shop and graduate without involving Mom or Dad in the decision.

Rhonda's mother got me a job at an electronics company after graduation. In very little time, I was the production floor supervisor. With Mom babysitting Lucy, I hired Linda to work with me for a short time until Rhonda's mother helped get her a job assembling circuit boards from home.

My bare feet began to hurt badly from a planter's wart. I asked Dad for advice on how to alleviate such pain. With his keen eye and his old-school knowledge of how to heal anything, I allowed him to carve it out with his pocketknife. That thing grew 200 heads or more, and I consulted a professional. With a loud gasp from the doctor and a complete surgical procedure, I was finally pain-free and resorted to modern-day medicine after that point.

Focusing on creating a home life with Opey and working on a career, I found little time to visit the homeplace throughout the week. Linda and I talked frequently on the phone, and I always stopped in to see the others on Sundays. The girls were all growing up, and David and Billy Joe were best of pals. Vickie and Berta were dating and driving, and the creek seemed to have little to offer. The front yard resembled a store parking lot. The traffic up and down the lane seemed nonstop as Reva and Bam practiced driving the old junker car. The constant stir of dust from the lane was frowned upon and lay heavy on all the cars and everything around.

Mom could fish with us often while Kay and Donna chased Lucy, who was quite adventurous and stumbled about on the creek rocks.

Linda, even as a mother, still craved the excitement of the creek and, during the flood season, called me for our annual raft ride to town, something we had started years earlier. It was funny thinking back at how she talked me into such a stupid thing.

We would spend half the morning blowing up a four-man orange raft using a tire pump. We would launch it at the end of our footpath into the creek, which was flooded from bank to bank, and tell Mom to pick us up in our small town in thirty minutes.

We never wore helmets or life jackets and never even owned a paddle for the raft. It was a fast and exhilarating ride and never punctured the raft on the many trees the rough water would thrust us into.

Linda would laugh about going down the creek without a paddle, and I sat still, holding the handles for dear life.

The others do this now with their children on tubes and full safety gear, launching from upstream and stopping at home.

Chapter 24

Dad's best friend, Gray, still frequented the house often. He loved all of us as his children. Having no children of his own, he would often bring a young kid named Scott from his city neighborhood with him to enjoy the country and play with all of us. In the winter, they would come down to shoot guns and rabbit hunt with Danny. Danny wasn't so big on the creek thing like me and Linda, but would tag along at times. Scott was a few years younger than Linda and I; he enjoyed the creek, fishing, and turtle hunting. He was always with us on the many frog-gigging expeditions at the end of the summer.

One early August day, Scott got his driver's license and stopped to visit Linda and me. Linda and Gary visited the house every day since Lucy enjoyed playing there. I, on the other hand, was always busy with work and would visit on Sundays, so I missed his visit. He spent the entire day fishing and messing around the creek with Linda and the others. At dark, Gary and Linda left, and Donna went home with them for the night to help Linda with Lucy.

Vickie, Berta, and Reva said their "goodbyes" to Scott as they headed out for the evening. Before Scott left, Bam and Kay talked him into a quick ride to the store for a pop, and David tagged along to get a candy bar. Assuming they would be back shortly, Mom went inside with Billy Joe to get ready for bed.

At the store, Bam and Kay met friends. They got in their car with David and told Scott to go home, assuring him it was fine. During a quick joy ride, the driver lost control and wrecked the car. Mom woke up early morning to a knock on the door from a police officer with information of a horrific car accident that left David dead, Bam hospitalized, and Kay being treated for a broken arm.

Vickie, Berta, and Reva drove to tell Linda the news as my phone rang. Mom, on the other end, cried and said, "David is dead! Bam is in the hospital from a car accident. Get there now! Your dad is on the way from the junkyard. It's not good."

Hanging up the phone, I shuddered at what I just heard and questioned if it was for real. Throwing on clothes, I screamed through the house for Opey to get up and drive me to the hospital since I was shaking too badly. I remember the air being icy cold for this time of year and the fog lying heavy as he drove through the curvy back roads to the hospital while thinking, *This was an absolute nightmare.*

We, as kids, had never experienced death before. Mom and Dad shielded us from such loss growing up until then, and our carefree life, as we know it, changed after that day drastically.

We buried David (age eleven) atop a hill in the cemetery of our small town while praying for Bam (age fourteen), who was on life support at the time. Despite medical advice to pull the life support plug, Bam passed two weeks later on her own and was buried beside little David.

The hurt and pain we all experienced was unimaginable. Dad was beside himself with anger, and his protective hand weighed heavy on the others still left at home. The accident was rarely discussed, even with Kay, and many questions about that night remain unanswered.

Present Day

I found myself stopped at a stop sign that early morning, bawling like a baby and swearing out loud.

I had done this all before. It seemed as if I had just driven a hundred miles toward home, remembering, and still wasn't home yet.

It was so foggy driving through the curvy back road, and the air had that same icy chill to it for an early August morning.

I left everyone at the nursing home to sit with Linda, including my mother, who was asleep in her car. I came home to get some rest.

I cried for her pain to be losing a daughter soon, as I did many years ago when little David and Bam died from that car accident. I had that same sick feeling in my gut.

"Could I do more?" I questioned.

I would soon lose my best friend, and it took me this long to realize the loss my sisters and little brother must've felt when they lost their best friends in that car wreck.

I had buried myself in work and my own life and pushed that pain away back then. Thinking back, Linda never displayed any loss, for she never truly let them go. She held onto the memories and visited with them while fishing at the creek.

I asked her once if she heard the giggles and laughter down there as we sat on the bank trying to catch that bass years later.

She looked over at me and said calmly, "They never left."

Then, she just smiled and went back to studying her fishing line. She was remembering that fun day at the creek, I suppose. She knew more than I did, and I wish I had slowed down and taken the time.

I wiped the pools of tears from my eyes and proceeded on home, looking back at what once was...

Chapter 25

Most of us managed to move out and have children of our own now and frequent the family home quite often. It was especially on Sundays and holidays, some more than others. After the car accident, something always seemed missing, but the void soon filled with the laughter and spirit of all of our small children. It was comforting to see a small baby in Mom's arms all the time and the front yard riddled with bits of paper and cups again.

Billy Joe, still in high school, and Danny were working from the garage now, and Dad was merely supervising. It was the hangout for many stories, beer drinking, and a lot of tinkering. Most of the work was done on the family cars and was, of course, non-paying. Our toys were motorized ATVs and dirt bikes. Our walking paths were now wide dirt tracks. An old junker car, truck, or jeep was still available to transport us and our fishing poles to the creek.

Linda, Berta, her boyfriend, Skip, Billy Joe, and I decided to venture to Walter's Pond one Sunday on Easter with our children and try to spark an interest in them for adventure at such a young age. We knew that they would tire out. We laughed at how we heard it all before, about 15 years prior.

Linda was still catching turtles and crawdads, skipping rocks, and searching for things of interest. I was merely following and keeping an eye on all the children and trying not to get hurt myself. Berta was carrying a small cooler with six beers, like Grandma, who had recently passed, and basked in the sun as we treaded along the edge of the creek.

The past floods had filled most of our swimming spots with gravel. A gravel company was removing it to ensure the water stays within the banks during the upcoming rainy season. The high banks were covered with large broken slabs of concrete to prevent erosion, and without the fertile dirt, the swallows were gone. Our shallow crossing was still there, and to our grownup selves, the creek appeared to be merely a small stream of water.

We carried the children over the other crossings since the water was so cold this early in the year and decided to skip the turtle pond. We walked up the tractor road and pointed out the grove of large vines to the kids, who disappointingly showed no interest. We reached the old metal gate and had to climb over and laugh at the children as they shimmied under, as we once did. The path up the hill to the pond was still quite visible, yet the grassy field was a little overgrown and displayed an array of small spring flowers due to the absence of the big cows.

Not much had changed atop the hill at the pond, and it was still quite peaceful. We resorted to picnicking on Easter candy rather than our peanut butter sandwiches as Linda and I told them the story about the big old cow. The way we described it had the children looking for that long-horned cow, ready to run. It was amazing how fresh my memory of that day was.

Being short on time and the kids whining about how far away we were from home, we chose the old field shortcut to save their little legs and bare feet to get back before dinner.

It was fun to take time to go back, and we talked about doing it every Easter. Sad to say, we never took the time, and I'm not really sure as to why.

Chapter 26

Present Day

I woke early in the afternoon after the long night and got dressed, still thinking of Linda. How she spent the whole day saying "goodbyes" to the many who came to visit with such grace, style, and dignity. She comforted them while she lay and endured so much pain. Her strength was unimaginable, yet she was dying? How was that possible?

I still think to myself, *I could never do that. I never could do anything she did, and how she never changed throughout her life.*

I had listened to her tell her daughters her last wishes and how she wanted to go fishing with Bam and David by Tuesday. Tuesday was the anniversary of the accident, and after Rhonda and I were stolen off the side of the road so many years ago, she was always on time, if not an hour early. Even now, I see her following through. I wanted to tell her to stick around, but I didn't. I couldn't be selfish, and I could tell she was tired.

She said to me the night before, "Go to work, and don't worry about me."

Then asked, "What time do you get off?"

I replied, "Two, but I don't have to go in."

"Yeah, go in and work," she said.

I could not go to work that day. I made plans for my daughter-in-law to drive me up to see her. As I sat at my desk waiting, I found myself in a blank state, a motionless, frozen sense of being for many minutes.

My daughter-in-law came and asked, “Joann, are you alright?”

She had asked many, many times before I heard her and snapped back to reality.

Slowly turning my head toward her, I said, “She is gone. She just sucked the life right out of me. I felt her leave,” as tears streamed down my face.

The phone rang.

I glanced at the clock. It was two.

I thought to myself after hanging up the phone. *She was in control. She saved my heart from the hell I would feel of watching her pass, and for that, I thank her.*

Now, I will never again get the chance to sit with my big sister and laugh at the crazy things we did growing up. We will not be able to talk about the many secrets we shared and the trouble she skillfully evaded.

As I move on and deal with the trials life tends to present—love, hardship, grief, and health—I appreciate her advice to me that day at the creek fishing.

If I take a minute from life and go to the creek, I can hear the laughter and giggles down there when I stop. I just smile and remember, “They never left.”

Made in the USA
Columbia, SC
22 July 2024

a7fe2e2c-b65f-46d8-85fe-c5076f20782dR01